CHASING TRUTH

BOOK 2 OUTLASTING SERIES

LK MAGILL

FIRST HALE PRESS

Chasing Truth/ LK Magill – 1st ed.

Ebook ISBN 978-1-7336155-6-3

Paperback ISBN 978-1-7336155-7-0

Hardcover ISBN 978-1-950928-06-4

DEDICATION_

To God, for allowing me to write another.

ACKNOWLEDGMENTS_

I am so lucky to be surrounded by family, and friends who I count as family. I would be unable to create in this way without their constant support.

Ali (for your 2am texts and enthusiasm)

Sara Mae (for lending me your amazing middle name and providing such consistent feedback)

Jenna (my soul mate that isn't a guy, lol - for your honesty)

Mom (artist extraordinaire, therapist, financial backer, sympathizer)

Dad (maybe my biggest fan)

Kathy (how'd I get so lucky as to have you for a step-mom?)

Greg (brother, warrior, friend)

PROLOGUE_

THIS IS BOOK 2 IN A RAPID READER SERIES AND IS MEANT TO be read in order.

If you haven't already, please make sure to read OUTLASTING AFTER, Book 1 in the Outlasting Series, first.

Otherwise, enjoy!

IT WAS DARK. A SCATTERING OF STARS COULD BE SEEN overhead, partially hidden behind a shifting cover of clouds. Despite the hour, Cole could still see the disarray playing out all around him. They had a half moon tonight, and it was unforgivably bright.

Looking down, Cole stroked one hand over Hannah's golden hair. She was balled up at his feet, hands covering her ears, trying to hide from the screaming.

And it wasn't the other woman that called to her. No, she had stopped awhile ago. It was the guy who'd stabbed Ryder. The noises he made… well, they were otherworldly. Liam had been at him for hours. And even though the sounds were old news to Cole, he still recognized what a terrible thing it was to hear. Even if the man suffering deserved every second of it, he was still human.

"Well?" Cole asked, letting his gaze fall to the scene in the snow.

Ryder was limp, still belly down with a seeping slush of crimson surrounding him. Like a snow angel, Cole thought, or really a blood angel.

Ace was working alongside the woman, the one who knew Hannah's name. She had said she was a nurse and from what Cole could tell, it seemed she was, or had been, or whatever.

She was thin, so thin from an obvious lack of food, and her bright red hair was tattered and filthy. The clothes that covered her were in the same state of neglect, all ripped and stained. But she had shoes on her feet, which was more than Hannah had when he'd found her.

At Cole's question, the redhead's intelligent hazel eyes swiveled up to meet his and she huffed a breath. Indignant. She's got attitude, he realized. No wonder she has fresh bruises all over her pretty face, she didn't let them break her.

"He needs blood," the woman said. "Do you know what type he is?"

"Type A," Davey answered. His mouth moved but he was still out of it. Kneeling in the snow, he just stared down at the lifeless form of his little brother.

"You telling me you've got blood stored somewhere?" Cole's eyes narrowed, but he knew the answer.

This shit hole didn't have refrigeration, no one did, that was a thing of the past. There were no more hospitals, no blood banks, no ambulances or emergency surgeries. Ryder had been stabbed five times in the lower back, just beneath his damn bullet proof vest. He was bleeding to death, and there wasn't anything they could do to stop it.

"Who's type A?" Ace's voice cracked, then he began fumbling around in his medic kit.

He had carried the bag everywhere they went for the past three years, everywhere since their desertion. No one was allowed to touch it and you practically had to sever a limb before Ace would consider using it. But here he was now, up to his elbows in bloody gauze and empty syringes.

"I am." Davey exhaled suddenly, seeming to wake from his stupor. "I'm Type A. We're the same."

"You sure?" Ace was pulling out an IV line, ripping open a sterile needle. "Absolutely 100% the most sure you've ever been?"

"I'm sure." Davey nodded.

And then the nurse was crouching down beside Ace. She was picking carefully through the kit, taking out sterile wipes and Ace wasn't freaking out. He was talking to her. They were forming a plan.

Cole's eyes drifted up to check their surroundings once more. They couldn't stay out here, not in the cold, not in the open like this. Not after gunning down five men and continuing to torture a sixth.

If there was anyone at all around, they would be coming. Coming carefully if they had half a brain, but coming nonetheless. To see what was left over. To see what they could take.

"Can we move him?" Cole asked.

Ace stilled momentarily. The nurse, however, continued in her progress.

She knelt in front of Davey and motioned for him to lie flat beside his brother. Rolling up his sleeve, she cleaned a spot on his arm, and then turned to do the same for Ryder.

After inserting a needle into both of them, blood began to flow. It filled the tube attached between the two men, transferring life. Could this work? Cole didn't know.

He didn't know anything about it. That had never been his job. His job was to keep them together, safe and on point. Right now they were together, that was all.

"Well?" Cole was losing his patience, and it made him sound like he didn't care. But that was part of getting shit done, a part of you had to not care. "We can't stay out here in the snow. The cold will get him if nothing else."

"Alright," Ace relented. "We can move him, but we'll need help. A backboard of some kind, then we can carry him or drag him maybe. Where do you want to go?"

"Back to the trailers. We'll have to stay there tonight."

The nurse flinched, and it wasn't lost on Cole. The trailers down the hill were a house of horrors for her. Certainly, she didn't want to march right back in. But there was just no way around it. So Cole ignored her reaction, and lifted his eyes to find Chan.

He'd already been back and forth to the trailers a number of times. Chan was the one that found the key to the cage the women were in, and he'd brought a few blankets back. One to lay over Ryder and the other to wrap around the second woman. She was just a tiny bird of a thing, with pale skin and black hair.

Since their release, she hadn't said a word, nor had she looked at anyone. The nurse had called out to her once, but the woman hadn't responded. Her name was apparently Lena, and she sat with her back to everyone, head tilted against the outside of the cage.

"Chan." Cole shifted as Hannah continued to lean back against his legs, eyes squeezed shut. "Tell Liam he's got to cut it short. We need him."

But just as Chan was giving him a nod, the strangest thing happened. The tiny bird Lena, got to her feet. She turned to face Cole, all the while clutching the tan blanket around her shoulders. A pair of bright blue eyes locked with his, but only briefly before darting away. It was as if she could hardly stand to look at him, or any other man for that matter. Her voice was firm though and something in the tone struck a nerve with him.

"I'll go," she said. "I'll go make it stop."

And then she was moving towards the concrete building, just as another long howl echoed from behind the closed wooden door. Hannah shuddered against his legs and Cole continued to stroke at her hair.

Liam was doing exactly what Cole had asked him to. He was making the asshole feel it; feel all of it, and that took time. Time they no longer had.

As Cole watched the woman drift away in the dark, her steps were haphazard, like she wandered a bit to the left, then a bit to the right. She wasn't all there. Cole should probably stop her. He shouldn't allow this woman to interrupt Liam. It could be dangerous, you never knew what state you'd find him in.

But something in the fleeting pierce of Lena's blue eyes stayed his hand. She wanted to see. She wanted to watch one of her captors as a victim. So instead, Cole made a compromise, and gestured to Chan.

"Go with her," he directed, before kneeling down beside Hannah and coaxing a hand from her ear. "It's all going to be over now and I really need your help, Han. Will you help me?"

It took Hannah a few seconds before her big brown eyes focused on Cole. He let his fingers drift down her cheek, then under her chin where his thumb rubbed slowly along her jawline. She had scared him, scared him bad, and that was not easily done.

Remembering the dread that pulsed through him at the sight of her had his jaw tightening even now. She shouldn't have been here. But here she was, and he still didn't know how it had happened.

He and Chan had been outside the smaller of the two trailers, the one tucked a bit below and further back in the trees. They had circled it first, peeking through the windows to spy the absolute destruction that lay inside.

The furniture had been stripped out, with only the bare linoleum flooring and a few useless light fixtures remaining. There was a mattress on the floor in the far end and a few buckets. One man was sleeping fully clothed on the bed. The other was hunched over, carving something into the floor with a knife.

Cole had taken his position, glanced at Chan, and received a nod. Then they waited. At the sound of Liam's whistle, they opened the door easy as you please, walked in and shot the bastards before they even had a chance to move. But then they heard a mix of gunfire and shouting from the larger trailer.

Running in the snow, rifle poised, breath controlled, it had been a rush. It brought Cole back to those years living for the next mission. For a chance to get even, for a chance to avenge his family. But no matter how many buildings they torched, bombs they set, or bodies they left stacked in the street, it never did seem to pacify.

And when this rescue mission had gone south, it had been right quick, as they usually will do. Over the sound of gunshots, they heard the female screaming. At that point three more men lay dead in the trailer and it became painfully obvious they were missing one.

That's when Cole and Chan broke and started running. They heard Davey yelling and when they got to the rise, he was kneeling in the snow with Ryder cradled in his arms. Hannah skidded to a stop moments later. What was she doing there in the middle of everything? Cole's chest had constricted then, so tight that he still didn't feel comfortable breathing deep.

Not even now, hours later.

"I don't know her," Hannah whispered, so softly Cole

had to concentrate on her lips to make out the words. "She knows me, but I don't know her."

"It's okay," Cole whispered back, but let his eyes dance to the nurse, still taking blood from Davey.

"Don't leave me alone with her," Hannah pleaded. "I don't know her, Cole. I don't know her."

CHAPTER TWO_
LIAM

Liam was still straddling the other man, but he didn't need to anymore, not really. The concrete building had fallen to darkness, with only a shaft of moonlight peeking through a rotted hole in the roof. It was just enough for Liam to see by but he didn't need it to keep working. He could do this work by feel, even with the man shaking beneath him.

And it wasn't from fear either. It wasn't a tiny trembling. The guy's entire body was vibrating. Shock. The weak bastard was in shock already and Liam knew he wouldn't make it much longer.

In the palm of his hand, Liam held onto the bullet that either Ryder or Davey had sunk into him. There had been two shots though, so the second one must have gone high and wide. Unfortunately, that's what would probably cost Ryder his life. That and the fact no one went to check that the guy was dead. It was sloppy.

Liam gritted his teeth at the thought, and drew his blade methodically down the length of one arm. The man howled but barely twisted. His body was shutting down, losing the battle at life. Liam had removed the man's jacket a while ago, not wanting to cut it up. Winter clothing was scarce so they would strip everything useful from this hellhole before leaving, even the clothes off the dead men's backs. Boots, too.

Liam brightened at the prospect.

"What's behind the wall?" He asked.

"I don't know, I don't know, I don't know."

The man moaned, shaking his pitiful head side to side, causing blood to drip this way and that. It had been the same answer to the same question asked a dozen ways, all accompanied by the loss of fingers or flesh. Liam wasn't getting anywhere, which meant that the man was likely telling the truth.

Maybe he didn't know what was behind the wall, but he *had* been able to tell Liam how to get there, what it looked like and the general rumors surrounding it.

The thing that most intrigued Liam was the fact that the rumors hadn't traveled further south. The locals were just too damn scared. Scared of what, though? Or maybe it was a who?

Liam wiped his knife off on the man's tattered shirt and contemplated. Someone was coming. The skin on the back of his neck stood on end and a ripple of awareness washed over him. It was in the crunch of snow, the shift in the air, the energy that pushed its way closer.

Glancing down into the man's face, Liam noted tears leaking from the corners of his eyes.

"Don't go anywhere," Liam whispered, then got up and stood in the corner closest to the door.

It was a tiny box of a room that had once housed the well pump for the property. Those parts had long since been dismantled and so all that was left was the cold hard floor and the imposing concrete walls.

Logically, Liam knew it had to be one of his team coming to fetch him, but that small voice inside his head, the one that had managed to keep him alive, said to wait and watch. So he did. And what he saw when the door pulled open was a surprise.

A slight figure, wrapped in a tan blanket, stood on the threshold and looked down at the man moaning on the floor. It was a woman. The ends of her dark hair were mostly tucked inside the blanket, but a gust of wind picked up a strand and blew it about her face. Outside, the darkness was almost as intense as inside the small structure, but the half moon did provide some back light.

Liam held his breath, knife gripped loosely in one hand and observed her. She couldn't rip her eyes away from what she saw sprawled on the floor, and after a beat, Liam saw her lips purse, then begin to quiver.

"You shouldn't be seeing this," Liam said softly, and the woman jumped visibly, but did not take a step back.

"I want to see," the woman's voice was quiet, and just behind her, Liam caught sight of Chan.

"Time's up?" Liam asked, lifting his voice to his teammate, but not shifting his eyes from the girl.

"Yeah," Chan answered.

"Cole approve this?" Liam gestured to the woman, who finally turned to make eye contact.

"I have to see," she said, and in her eyes, Liam witnessed the reason.

Ducking his head, Liam gestured for her to move further in. He typically didn't share this sort of thing, especially not with a civilian, and a damaged fucking one at that. But if Cole had let her come this far, then who was Liam to stop her? Anyway, he would finish the guy quick and she could watch, but he wasn't going to turn his back on her.

Glancing over his shoulder, Liam noted Chan standing still in the doorway, his face revealing nothing, as usual. Chan had witnessed this before, maybe twice, but it had been out of necessity. They needed code or some shit from the guys Liam had been working.

"Ryder?" Liam asked.

"Not yet," Chan answered the unspoken question, *was he dead?* Because that would change how Liam wanted to do it. After a beat Chan added, "Close though."

Frowning, Liam returned his attention to the task at hand. With the light from the moon behind him, Liam could see the full extent of damage he had done to the man and so could the woman who now cowered in the far corner. What had happened? She had been so sure just a moment before.

Liam shrugged the concern off. This is exactly why he liked to work alone. He didn't have to worry about what the others thought of him and in the end they all got what they wanted. Whether it be intel, vengeance, or otherwise.

"You can still leave," Liam murmured to the woman as he placed a boot over the man's thigh. The fucker had actually started to roll to one side, like he had a chance in hell of getting away.

"No," the woman panted her words now. "I- I- need to make sure that he's dead."

Liam paused, letting his eyes flick to the woman's strained face, then back to the bleeding blubbering lump on the ground. After a beat, he tossed his knife into the air, flipping the blade over once before catching it easily in his hand. The weight, the balance, it was just right. And that was what this kill was really all about, right? Balance.

"You mean you have to see *him* die in particular?" Liam asked.

"*Him*." The woman's breath caught in her throat and she nodded.

"Do you want to do it?"

Liam flipped the knife in the air once more, this time catching the blade side carefully in the palm of his hand. He held the handle out in her direction, watched her blue eyes track to it and hold.

"Because I'll help you do it," Liam added. "If you want."

CHAPTER THREE_
HANNAH

Snow crunched beneath her boots, the horses snorted, and Hannah worked hard not to be sick. Beneath the cover of towering pines and twisting oaks, it was so dark. The partial moon threw some light but the branches obscured it, causing shadows to shift and dance on the ground.

If Cole hadn't been just ahead of her, leading his horse and the mule, then Hannah wasn't sure she could have done it. Though logically, she had walked the woods at dark more times than she could count, she had never done it in the snow. And never with the sounds of a dying man echoing in her head.

He was dead now, the man, he had to be. Cole had walked her far away from the bad place. They had returned to the cart, unhitched the horses and mule, then stocked up on food and sleeping bags. Now they were walking the animals back.

Hannah felt the cold twist of rope in her hand. Glancing behind her, she looked up into the face of Liam's horse. He flared his nostrils and exhaled a breath. It smelled decidedly of warm hay. The scent, for some unknown reason, made her feel better, if only slightly.

"After we crest the hill, I want you to close your eyes," Cole said.

He had turned his head to one side, his breath rising from his mouth as he talked. She could just see the puff of steam in a shaft of light thrown by the moon. For a moment Hannah wondered what he didn't want her to see, but then she was nodding her head and resolving not to care.

They emerged from the forest into the clearing and hiked to the top of the small slope. Just before she crested the rise, Cole stopped and took her hand. They would walk side by side now, him leading not only his gray and the mule, but Hannah and the bay, too.

Obediently, she shut her eyes and did her best not to stumble as they started their descent towards what she knew to be the concrete building and the metal cage. With her eyes closed, her other senses began to fill in the gaps in her surroundings. She could smell the frost on the air, feel the slope flatten out, hear the stomp of horse hooves and creak of saddles.

Inhaling through her nose, Hannah sorted out the smells that surrounded her. There was moisture in the air, but it hung there absently, with no rain drops or snow flakes falling. And the stench of decay, it was like tasting iron in your mouth. Strange, she thought, when had she tasted iron? *Iron is a sort of metal.*

Then her brain was flashing and she was standing inside a room. It was bright with overhead lights and there were people, so many people. Looking down, Hannah saw her own body. She was wearing clean jeans that narrowed at her ankle and fit low on her hips. A pair of black flip flops were on her feet and her toe nails... they were painted plum purple.

The people all around her were milling about, pacing along the walls and into the center of the space. No one was sitting. There were no children, no old people.

She could hear the murmur of questions. *Why are we in here? I thought this was supposed to be for our safety? Did they take your phone? They took mine.* And Hannah patted her own pockets and realized she too had been robbed of her precious device.

Then someone was yelling. *Hey, you can't just lock us in here! We have rights! You can't just take our things!* And more people were grumbling and the mood inside the room changed.

Let us out! Let us out! Someone was screaming and the panic was like lighting a match inside a powder keg. People began shoving, moving and running.

Hannah was pushed against the far wall where her back hit hard and her breath caught in her chest. Then she had her hands up, trying to protect her body, trying to stop the force of people around her. They were clawing at the walls, smashing into each other, someone was on the ground, getting trampled.

Hannah screamed and found herself being carried along in the mass of bodies until she was pressed up against a long stretch of iron bars. She hadn't seen them from the back of the room where she'd been standing. And facing them now, she stuck her hands through, wanting help. *Please help me.*

But the bodies kept squeezing her against the metal, and her mouth came down against the bars. The tangy taste of iron rushed over her lips and tongue. Iron equals death. Death by crushing in a prison cell.

"I told you not to look!" Cole was shouting at her. "Close your eyes, Han! Close your eyes!"

And then Hannah was sucked back into the present, and her eyes were open and she was screaming. The horses were stomping and scattered all around. Wet snow was seeping into the seat of her pants.

She was sitting on the ground with Cole crouched before her, shaking her shoulders. Reaching a hand up to her mouth, she brushed her fingers against her lips, so sure there would be blood dripping there. Blood from the iron bars digging into her, but there was nothing.

"Damn it." It was Liam's voice, and he was standing over them.

"Get her inside." Cole's eyes darted over her face. "I'll get the horses."

Then Hannah was looking up into Liam's face and just past his head there was the metal cage. It was the one that housed the women, though they weren't inside it anymore.

Squinting her eyes in the dark, Hannah tried to focus. Her mind still felt slow and raw, but there *was* a figure inside the cage. And just as Liam gathered her to him and lifted her into his arms, she realized what she was looking at.

It was the bad man. He was hanging upside down from one ankle inside the cage. His body was grotesque in its position, one leg folded awkwardly down, his arms limp, his mouth and eyes open. There was blood, so much blood, in dried trails all over him. And in the slight breeze, his body was swaying, rotating slowly around.

"I'm sorry," Liam whispered. "He was dead before I hung him like that, I'm sorry."

Hannah's breath hitched in her throat and her body began to tremble, but Liam turned quickly away and headed for the trailers. She had remembered again, she had a memory.

Hannah's heart tripped and her head rushed. It wasn't at all like the one of the doctor. That one was so mild. This one was the opposite. She could still feel the panic in her blood. Beads of sweat were bubbling out along her brow.

Why had she been in that prison cell? Because now she knew that's what it was. She could close her eyes and see it in her mind. The memories, once they came back, were so strong. It was like she could re-live them over and over if she wanted.

"I have to do it like that," Liam was talking, obviously thinking that the man's body is what had triggered Hannah's meltdown. "It's the only warning that men understand. It's the only way to keep the others from coming while we're here."

Opening her mouth, Hannah tried to speak, but no words came out. She wanted to tell Liam it was okay, wanted to tell him the real reason she had been screaming, but then they were at the trailer and he was calling for them to open the door.

There was light inside and warmth. A wood burning stove was positioned in the middle of one long wall and the grate was left open, a bright orange fire roaring inside.

Ryder's body lay on a long couch, belly down, with his head turned to one side. Davey was pacing the room, rubbing absently at his arm while Ace held two fingers to Ryder's neck and counted under his breath. That meant he was still alive right? If they were hovering around him, then Ryder was still alive.

"Hannah," a female voice called. It was the woman, the one from before, the nurse. "Hannah, are you okay? It's me, Flynn. Hannah, please. Where's Andy? What happened to him?"

Liam's hands were cradling her body and she felt him tighten reflexively before glancing down at her face. Try as she might, Hannah didn't recognize the woman called Flynn.

When she looked over at the redhead, she felt a touch of unease work its way through her. She didn't want to be left alone with her, she didn't want to talk to her, or even be near her. So Hannah gripped Liam's jacket in both of her hands and buried her face in his chest.

"Keep her away from me," Hannah whispered and felt Liam hug her tighter. "Don't leave me with her. I don't know her."

Cole had been under the impression that this shit show of a mission could not get any worse. Then he opened the door to the larger of the two trailers and stepped inside. The blast of heat from the fire hit him first, but it was the raised voices that washed over him in waves.

Eyes tracking, Cole stepped decidedly inside and swung the door shut behind him. The click of it locking did nothing to impact the argument playing out before him.

"What did you do to her?!" The nurse was shrieking, squared off in the far corner.

"Nothing," Liam replied. He was deadly calm, like he always was. Hannah was cowering on the floor just behind him, making every effort to disappear. "You just can't talk to her right now."

"That guy told me this was some kind of rescue." The nurse gestured to Davey who still looked glassy-eyed. "But we want out of here, and we're taking Hannah with us."

"Like hell you are." Liam folded his arms across his chest and scowled.

Cole couldn't help but heave an exasperated sigh. Liam was *so* diplomatic, he knew just what to say to put everyone at ease. Ha. Ha. Ha.

Just as the redhead opened her mouth to speak, the tiny bird girl Lena reached up and tugged at her sleeve. Cole watched the exchange of glances, the slight shake of her head. When the nurse bit down hard on her lip and swallowed the words she was about to say, Cole was forced to raise his eyebrows with interest.

But it wasn't something he could dwell on, not with Liam standing guard like a pit bull and Hannah crumbling behind him. Cole had to jump into the split second of silence before things devolved further.

"This *is* a rescue and both of you are free to leave whenever you'd like," Cole announced, causing all eyes to swivel towards him. "But before you make any decisions, I'd like to point out that it's below freezing outside. There's snow on the ground and you have shit for clothes and nothing in the way of food. I don't think you'll make it very far."

Pausing, Cole surveyed the room in silence. Ryder's back rose and fell ever so slightly. The kid was still sucking in air, that was good. Davey ran his shaky hands through his blonde hair and squeezed his eyes shut, face tilted towards the ceiling. He was going to crash soon, and hard.

The blood he had given his brother had drained him. Cole wondered if they'd need to do it again. And if so, when.

Then there were the women. The nurse with all her spitfire and fight, her face mottled with bruises. Then there was the little bird girl, so fragile. Her name was Lena. She blinked at him through drawn, tired eyes. She wasn't going anywhere.

And if *she* wasn't, then the nurse wasn't either. But there were obviously issues here Cole needed to address. Because Hannah was having a mental breakdown in the corner, and Liam was ready to throw down to protect her.

Before he could open his mouth to speak though, there came a series of abrupt knocks against the door. Chan was outside. He must have completed his last perimeter sweep. Cole unlocked the door and let him in.

Standing aside, he watched Chan heft bedroll after bedroll into the room, followed by the bags of food they had brought down from the cart. Once he was done, he too entered the now silent trailer, his black rifle in hand, and locked the door behind him.

Carefully, Chan leaned back against the door and waited. The man was nothing if not perceptive. He felt the tense silence probably better than anyone.

"Hannah has been through a lot." Cole let his gaze focus on the nurse who held his eyes without a hint of fear. "Now you say you know her and maybe she was your friend, but it doesn't look that way right now. Does it?"

The nurse's face scrunched up for the briefest moment before she dropped her head and looked down at Lena. The tiny bird gave up a sorrowful expression before the nurse lifted her head and replied, "I didn't say we were friends, exactly. But I never did anything to hurt her."

"Ah." Cole nodded, wondering what the full story was. "Well, it doesn't look like she wants to talk to you."

"But-"

"I'm willing to make you the same deal that I made with her," Cole interrupted. "You can stay with us and we will feed you. I promise that no one will hurt you. No one will touch you. But if you're going to stay, then you have to get along with everyone. Can you do that?"

"And we can leave whenever we want?" The nurse was tentative, testing.

"You can leave whenever you want."

"What about Hannah?"

"What about her?"

"Can she leave?"

"Hannah can leave, too… if she wants."

Cole said the words aloud, kept his expression honest and his eyes steady. But on the inside, his whole body felt the force of the lie. He would never be able to let Hannah go. Not with anyone, or for any reason. Cole would keep her, or die trying.

But the false promise he made was well received. It served to ease the tension in the room, making the nurse sit back down on the floor beside Lena. They huddled together just a few feet past the stove.

Slowly, the others began to move, too. Liam crouched down to face Hannah. His whispered words were like a humming in the air. Though Cole wanted to go to her, wanted to question her about the nurse and pull her into his arms, he knew that he couldn't. Not yet.

He would let Liam do the comforting this time while he took care of the business at hand. The business of managing his team, of getting them through the night and into the next morning. So, as purposefully as possible, Cole stooped over to paw through the bedrolls. He would need to begin laying them out. After a beat he felt Chan kneel beside him.

"Go take over for Ace. Let him rest," Cole instructed and Chan moved away to comply.

While Cole and Hannah had been gone fetching supplies, the others had ripped the front door off the smaller trailer and used it as a drag to transport Ryder to his current spot. They'd taken the bodies of the dead men around back and tossed them into a pile. Later, someone would have to go strip them of their boots and gear. Cole thought that someone was probably going to be him.

The building they now found themselves in was an old single wide trailer from back in the day. Like thirty years back if Cole was any good at guessing. The dark brown carpeted floor creaked underfoot and the ceiling looked like it leaked in a few spots. But the stove worked, so that was a plus.

Ryder was resting on the only remaining piece of furniture. If there had been a table, chairs, or even a countertop in the small kitchen area, they had long since been hacked apart and used for firewood.

After unrolling the sleeping bags on the floor, Cole rose

to standing and strode through the narrow space with a bag of food in his hand. He tossed a few pieces of hard tac to Liam, then another at Chan. Davey shook his head and waved the food away, but Ace accepted double his share with the understanding that he would get Davey to eat some.

Next on his list were the nurse and Lena. They were both surprised when he crouched down in front of them and held out the food. Feeding two more mouths would put a strain on the supply, but not by much. They had figured on having one of them by this point anyway.

"Thank you," the nurse said, while reaching out a hand to take the hard cornflour cake from him.

Lena didn't budge. After a beat, Cole set her portion on the floor and continued his progress through the room.

There were two outer doors to the trailer, one in the front and one in the back where the bedroom was. He needed to post watch by the back door, figuring whoever was awake with Ryder would be able to cover the front. The second issue he needed to address were window coverings. It would be too easy for someone to creep around and peek inside, just like they had done.

Pausing at the door to the bathroom, Cole eyed it appraisingly. It might do the trick if he chopped it into smaller pieces with the axe they'd brought. But then there was the matter of hanging it up to cover the windows.

Glancing about, Cole took stock of the sparse and filthy contents all around him. There was no way a hammer and nails were here, no way.

"Hey," Liam's voice sounded just next to him.

"You left her?" Cole craned his neck to look around his massive friend and spied Hannah tucked into her sleeping bag on the floor.

Her golden hair flowed from the open top, but her body was well hidden. Her face was turned away towards the corner of the room. Liam leaned back against the wall in the narrow hallway but kept his gaze fixed on Hannah, too. Even so, Cole could practically feel him rolling his eyes.

"Flynn couldn't make it three feet before I'd have her." Liam huffed a breath. "Besides, the second Hannah's head hit the floor she was out."

"Flynn?"

"The nurse."

"Oh." Cole paused, eyes swiveling back to the door in front of him. "You want a job?"

"I want to know why you sent that little girl into my interrogation," Liam fumed.

"Yeah." Cole nodded slowly, still distracted. "I was on the fence about that."

"On the fence?" Liam shifted his body to look quickly at Cole before returning his gaze to Hannah. "Is that how you're making decisions now?"

"You could have sent her back out," Cole reasoned, then added. "And she isn't a girl, I'd say she's about mid-twenties."

"Of all the-" Liam sucked in a breath and worked to keep his voice low. "Cole, we need you right now buddy.

We need you bad. If you haven't noticed, things aren't going so well."

"I've noticed." Cole glanced to the bedroom door once, then back to the bathroom door. "Could you rip these two doors off the hinges pretty easy?"

"What?"

"Take these two doors off." Cole stood back and gestured. "We can drag them into the living room and stand them up side by side to at least cover that big bay window. The smaller one above the couch still has an old curtain hanging, so for complete cover everyone is going to have to stay in the living room."

Liam pushed off the wall and stepped closer, running his fingers over the hinges before nodding. "Yeah, I can get the doors off."

"Great, do it then."

Cole opened the bedroom door and moved into the darkened space that was lit only by the moon and the stars. His eyes took in everything at once. The mattresses on the floor, the buckets of water, the twisted coils of rope and wire. House of horrors for certain, he thought.

"Listen, Cole…" Liam had followed him inside, was sucking in a breath, had more to say. But Cole already knew his concerns. He knew what Liam would say before he even said it and he didn't have time for this. Not now.

"We can't stay here past tonight," Cole cut him off, whirling to stare at his best friend in the dark. "That's all the time that Ryder gets to stabilize enough so we can transport him. If he lives until morning, then his ass has to be in that cart and we have to hope like hell the ride doesn't reopen his wounds. On top of that, the risk of infection is sky high. The chances of him dying a slow painful death far outweigh the chances of him living."

Cole paused, let that sink in, then went on.

"We've got to keep a close eye on Ryder all night, but Ace needs to sleep. Chan needs to sleep. Hell, we all need to sleep right now. But two guys have to be awake the whole night because this fucking shit house has two doors. Food, water, rest, and move. That's the priority, that's the plan. We're sitting ducks here and the horses are running short of feed."

"Okay." Liam exhaled slowly.

"Don't think I'm not worried sick about her, too. Don't think I don't want to interrogate the shit out of that nurse or Flynn or whatever her name is and find out exactly why Hannah is the way she is. Because I do, Liam. I do. But right now, Hannah can't be my priority. So that's where you come in. Go protect her, Lee. Go protect her so that I can do my job and we can all get out of here come first light. Okay?"

"Okay, Cole." Liam nodded his head. "Okay."

Every bump was agony. Walking alongside the cart, Liam could practically feel the stabbing in his own back as Ryder softly moaned. They had been on the road for over five days now and progress was slow, painfully slow. Lifting his eyes to the horizon, Liam noted the sun beginning its downward crawl. Night would be coming and they would need to make camp soon.

Beside him, Hannah picked her way carefully over the uneven ground. The hood of her black jacket was pulled up over her head but wisps of her golden hair fell forward, swaying and swirling with each step. Liam reached out briefly and tucked them back in.

Hannah didn't pause in her travels. Her arms were outstretched for balance and she kept her face downcast, pretending that her entire focus was necessary to navigate the terrain before her.

But Liam knew better. He knew the real reason she

didn't want to look up. And it was sitting right now in the cart, monitoring Ryder's status. It was Flynn. The nurse, with her searching stare and huffs of impatient breath.

She was always seeking Hannah. And up to this point everyone, including Liam, had been too damn distracted and, frankly, too tired to figure out why. All Liam had managed to do was run some pretty stout interference, which basically was just prolonging the inevitable.

Wherever he went, Hannah followed and Flynn was not allowed to go. They ate in different areas, slept on opposite sides of the cart and whenever they walked, Liam positioned his body between them. But now in the very midst of their travels, with Ryder somewhat stabilized and everyone settling into a routine, Liam was getting antsy.

He didn't like the way Hannah cowered when Flynn spoke, he didn't like it at all. It was time to get to the bottom of things, to get some clarity, to get some answers. But Liam had interrogated enough people to understand the delicate game that lay before him.

He couldn't question Flynn the way he would a soldier. No. He would have to be subtle, calculating and patient. This was all about trading information, knowing what to give away and what to keep. And of course, he would have to run his plan by Cole first so that he could assist when necessary.

A low whistle sounded somewhere behind them and all eyes turned to look. Speak of the devil, Liam thought. Here came Cole now, trotting up on his gray horse who was looking a bit thinner these days, despite the thickness of his winter coat. The feed was nearly gone and they still had at least four more days to go.

"How is he?" Cole asked, pulling up to survey the cart.

"Warm," Flynn answered, laying the back of her hand against Ryder's forehead.

"Fever?"

"Not yet."

Cole bobbed his head, then glanced up at the sky peeking through the pines. It was overcast, cloudy and cold. Liam sucked in a breath and rolled the air around on his tongue. No rain tonight, he judged. But that didn't mean it wasn't on its way.

"Let's keep pushing another hour, yet," Cole announced.

"He needs to rest, to drink more water," Flynn argued. "This much travel could kill him."

Cole narrowed his eyes and stared down at the little redhead for a beat. Liam could see his jaw working beneath his beard and tried not to grin. They had been a team for so long it was rare, like never happened rare, that anyone questioned Cole during a mission. But now this little addition kept fighting him at every turn. If Liam hadn't felt so defensive over her interactions with Hannah, he might have enjoyed the exchange more.

"Ace?" Cole asked finally, lifting his head to look at the man stomping out a trail in front of the mule.

"He's tough," Ace replied.

The team's medic didn't stop, didn't bother to turn around. They were all used to this sort of forced marching. It was nothing new and though their bodies still protested the lack of sleep, the minimal food and sparse water, their minds had been trained for it.

There was something to be said for conditioned familiarity. The guys could do this all day, everyday, until Cole said to stop. No question.

"An hour more then," Cole barked, and nudged his horse forward without so much as a backwards glance.

Liam dug around in his jacket pocket and pulled out his canteen. It was small, one he had come across years before, but the size was just right for this type of thing. Unscrewing the cap, he held it in front of Hannah's face.

After a beat, she reached out and took it, gulping down the contents greedily before wiping the back of her hand over her pretty mouth. Liam missed kissing that mouth, wanted to kiss that mouth right now in fact, but he didn't. When she handed his canteen back over, he took a brief sip before twisting the cap back on and shoving it deep into his pocket.

"You shouldn't do that," Ace called, now that Cole had disappeared from sight. "You shouldn't question him like that."

"Oh, is that not allowed here?" Flynn's retort was full of sass, just like her, all vinegar.

"You're lucky Davey wasn't around to hear it," Ace continued, still walking.

That had been the best assignment Cole had handed out yet. Davey was riding point on the bay horse, scouting their trail, picking the best path to pull Ryder through.

That way he didn't have to listen to his brother's suffering all day long.

"Maybe he should hear it," Flynn countered. "It's his brother right? He should have options for his care."

That's when Ace actually laughed. Like he had to stop and put his hands on his knees, type laugh. The mule paused too, waiting behind his leader. And so then did the rest of them. It was like a chain reaction. Liam and Hannah on one side, then Chan and Lena in the rear. All panting and silent, listening to Ace lose it for a minute.

When he caught his breath, he just shook his head and wiped a tear from his eye, then started walking again.

"Choice for his care?" Ace continued finally, breath puffing. "Woman, where have you been? There is no choice here."

"There's always a choice." Flynn refused to give up. "He could rest Ryder more, travel less. It could be the difference between life and death."

Ace whirled around on her then, forcing everyone to come to a sudden halt once more. Pointing an accusing finger at Flynn, his words were uttered through gritted teeth.

"You want a choice between life and death?" Ace's brown eyes flashed. "If you plant that seed of doubt in Davey's head, then we are all dead. Do you understand that? If he thinks Ryder can't travel, then he will stay here with his brother and watch him die. The rest of us will be forced to split. With less men there are less guns, less eyes, less protection. There are others in these hills, can't you feel them looking?"

"N- No-" Flynn glanced up into the forest, swallowed hard.

"Keep your hair under your hood and do not question Cole. Got it?"

"Yeah." Flynn's hands raced under her hood but her ragged red hair was still tucked safely inside of it. "Got it."

Silence fell amongst them as they continued to walk. Liam tucked his tongue in his cheek to keep from snickering. That last part about others watching them was pretty damn genius. No one had followed them. No eyes tracked their progress, Liam was sure.

But that didn't mean it couldn't happen. Up around the next bend or down in the next valley, they could meet with other men. Cole and Davey were doing their best not to let it happen, but some things were unavoidable. Fate, maybe.

Liam felt a slight tug on the sleeve of his jacket and glanced down at Hannah. What Ace had said had frightened her. He could see it clearly in those round doe eyes.

Giving his head a slight shake, he mouthed the word *no* and watched her visibly relax. Don't worry, Liam thought, even if there were eyes, I'd never let anyone touch you.

CHAPTER SIX_
HANNAH

THE FOREST ROSE UP ALL AROUND THEM. OVERHEAD, SHE watched a drifting bank of fog seeping in to obscure the tips of the pine trees. No wind. Hannah exhaled a tired breath and watched the puff of air rise above her head before dissipating.

It was frigid, but there wasn't any snow on the ground up here. They'd hiked all day steadily up the side of a mountain. But now the sun had set and darkness was folding down like a blanket. It was time to make camp, wasn't it? It had to be time.

Hannah's legs trembled and her feet were so sore. Up ahead, she could just make out the dip of a valley. Starting tomorrow, they would begin their descent into it. She wondered how much longer they had to go. How much further until they reached the safety of the compound? Would Ryder make it? The thought left a constricting ache in her throat and if she had any moisture to spare, she could probably have produced a few tears.

"Here's good." Cole's voice broke into her thoughts. Adjusting her gaze, Hannah watched him dismount from his horse. "We can make fire tonight."

No one spoke but Hannah could feel the relief all around her. They hadn't had a fire since they'd started traveling. The sky had been too clear. Now because of the fog they could chance some smoke. The thought of warmth made her want to cry.

Liam moved away from her side then to tend to his horse so that Davey could climb into the cart and check on his brother. Normally, Hannah would have followed him but her knees gave out and instead she slumped down in the dirt. Her body was so done.

Although she knew staying close to Liam was the only thing that kept Flynn at bay, Hannah just couldn't take another step. And though the redhead was a bold one, Liam was positively fierce. He never said much, but the vibes he put out were all dark and imposing.

Plus, they had all listened to what he'd done to that man back in the bad place. Covering your hands with your ears will only do so much to dampen that type of suffering. The memory sent a brief chill through Hannah even now, but she shoved the thoughts aside and kept her eyes focused on the rocky ground.

If only she could remember why she should fear Flynn. The mix of feelings Hannah got whenever she heard the woman speak were confusing at best. It wasn't that she felt physically threatened by Flynn, it was an underlying feeling that told Hannah not to trust her, not to speak to her, to avoid her. It was something so deep and ingrained that Hannah's lack of specific memories made the feeling even more acute.

"Hi," a woman's soft voice uttered the single word.

Shifting her gaze to the right, Hannah spotted Lena drop down to her knees just beside her. The woman was like a delicate porcelain doll. Her skin was so smooth and white with big blue eyes and raven black hair that hung down like a curtain.

Everything about Lena was subdued, from the way she clasped her hands in front of her to the way her face tilted always to the side and away. Even now, she gave Hannah her profile and said nothing, though she was close enough for Hannah to reach out and touch without the need to extend her arm.

For a few moments, Hannah let her gaze flow over Lena. Did she have any feelings when it came to her? Any memories? After hesitating just a beat, Hannah shifted her hand and laid it ever so carefully on top of the other woman's.

The gesture was meant to a be a light testing one, but the tightness with which Lena clung back was surprising. Immediately she interlaced her fingers in Hannah's own before laying her head decidedly on Hannah's shoulder. It was the most physical contact Hannah had seen the other woman give, even with Flynn.

"Thank you," Lena exhaled the words as Hannah sucked

in a sharp breath. "For coming to find us. I know you're angry with Flynn for what she did, but you can't still blame her for it, can you? And Andy went back for you in the end anyway, right? So can't you forgive her?"

Hannah's head began to swim and heat flushed her cheeks. What was she supposed to say? She had no idea what Lena was talking about.

Lifting her head, Hannah spied Cole on the other side of the cart, talking to Flynn. The two of them appeared to be involved in some sort of intense debate. But Lena took Hannah's silence as an answer and continued speaking quietly.

"The men here... do they hurt you?"

Hannah could feel Lena tense in preparation for the answer, and it made her soften just a fraction. This woman... she had been through so much. If Hannah didn't feel anything for her, then she was probably safe, right?

"No," Hannah replied, shaking her head slightly. "These are good men."

"Even the tall one?"

"You mean Liam?"

"Yes."

"He doesn't hurt women," Hannah qualified. She wasn't sure she could call him "good" anymore. Not after what he was so obviously capable of, though her feelings for him remained unchanged.

"What happened to Andy?" Lena's voice dropped even lower. Hannah had to strain to hear it. "Did Liam..."

"No." Hannah squeezed Lena's hand in reassurance. "Andy was gone before they found me."

"So he's dead?"

"Yes."

"Oh-" Lena began to sniffle just a little at the news. "Flynn is going to be so heartbroken. I mean we figured when he didn't come back with you that you were both dead, but seeing you gave us hope."

"I'm sorry." Hannah didn't know what else to say. Slowly, her head began to spin, her cheeks were flushing.

"Did you find Uriah?"

Lena lifted her eyes to lock with Hannah's then and the intense blue scrutiny was powerful... familiar. That name. Uriah. It began to pulse and throb inside Hannah's head, building with each thump of Hannah's heart.

Quickly, she tried to disentangle her fingers from Lena's, but the movement had the other woman frowning.

"Hannah Mae," Lena's voice raised. "It's like you don't even know me. What's going on?"

Hannah Mae. Hannah Mae. The name repeated itself and repeated itself, echoing around inside Hannah until she shoved decidedly away. Her head throbbed. The scar on her hand pulsed.

Scrambling back in panic, Hannah looked once more into Lena's eyes, so strangely worried now. Pushing up, she made a break for it. A break for the trees.

Running, running, she had to run. Had to get away.

. . .

"HANNAH MAE, DON'T YOU TRUST ME?" IT WAS ANDY'S VOICE talking and he was leading her down a narrow tunnel.

Light bulbs glowed overhead, making the silver metal of the walls shimmer. They passed camera after camera, but the little red lights on all of them were dark. It was cool down here, causing goosebumps to prickle along her skin.

Hannah knew she wasn't allowed inside the wall, but still, Andy had insisted she come.

"They voted me out, I'm not supposed to go." Hannah heard her own words echo dully as she tossed them at Andy's back.

He gave her a brief glance over his shoulder and smiled. "I promised your brother I would bring you, so I am."

Hannah frowned at that piece of information. Uriah had specifically told her to wait for him. Something about the whole situation seemed off, but then Andy was stopping at a large door. It was locked, with a digital reader just beside it. He turned to her and flipped open a knife, his eyes popping up to catch hers when she let go of a tiny gasp.

"I'm going to cut that thing out of you, then open this door and we're going to run. Okay? Run as fast as you can, Hannah Mae. Can you do that?"

Hannah rubbed at her right hand, the place where the microchip lay and her stomach did a summersault. "But Uriah said they don't know what it would do to me if it was taken out. Nobody's removed one yet and it makes me feel things sometimes. He thinks it could hurt me, hurt my mind."

Andy let his winning smile slip quickly to an expression of impatience. Hannah didn't even have time to take a step back before he was on her, slamming her to the ground, digging the knife into her hand. The hall echoed with the sounds of her screaming.

THE PLAN WAS A GOOD ONE, OR SO COLE HAD THOUGHT. Corner Flynn, start asking some questions, but away from Hannah, where she couldn't be triggered by any of the answers. Liam had come up with it. Of course he had.

Six days was a lot for an interrogator to wait while walking alongside his intended target. But he *had* waited, and so had Cole. Because in the end, the priority remained unchanged. Get them the hell back to the compound.

But it was nearing dark now, with some blessed fog to obscure them. Cole could let his guard down just a bit, turn his back on his duties for just a minute while the others set up camp. They were safe for now. Relatively so.

They hadn't been followed because Cole had spent most of the first day doubling back and covering their tracks. Even going so far as to break off some pine boughs and sweep the snow in a few places. That, combined with horse tracks leading in every sort of direction, should buy them the time they needed to get clear.

Then there was Ryder. He was clinging to life, just holding on for all he was worth. His sallow face, all taut with pain, was something awful to watch. When Cole had taken Ace aside, he confessed there was nothing more they could do except get him back.

He had a few more vials of penicillin but they were back at the compound. Hopefully, that would kill any infection that might be brewing. That being said, they were completely out of morphine. Ace had used it all on the kid already.

So, what could Cole do? Well, he could provide unending pain and the fastest route home possible. And that's just what he did. Only, he hoped Davey didn't split in two in the process. It was a lot for a man to take, watching your baby brother die.

"Hey, Flynn." Cole caught her as she swung a leg over the side of the cart. "I'd like a word."

"Alright." Flynn stepped gingerly down to the ground, balancing on wobbly legs that were cramped after a day spent caring for Ryder.

While the others walked, she gave him sips of water, fed him bits of food, and kept him as comfortable as possible despite the circumstances. Having a trained nurse around was a plus, definitely.

"I'm going to need you to start trusting me," Cole began, thinking of her constant questioning and knowing to get something you had to give, too.

"I know." Flynn bobbed her head, much to Cole's surprise. "Ace talked to me about it. Trust doesn't come easy for me."

"Look, everything I do is for the benefit of this team," Cole explained. "And as long as you're with us, that includes you. Now, I will do everything in my power to protect you along with everyone else here, but that involves you trusting me. Can you do that?"

"Yes," Flynn said, swallowing hard before choking out the next words. "Thank you. I appreciate your protection."

Glancing over the side of the cart, she let her gaze settle on Lena and Hannah. Cole followed her line of sight. The two women were holding hands, Lena's head was resting on Hannah's shoulder.

Cole tensed a moment, he couldn't help it. They had been so busy running interference on Flynn that he'd completely overlooked the little bird girl. She was so fragile and quiet that she hadn't seemed like a threat. Where was Liam?

Cole let his eyes dart around the camp and they came up empty, but he did catch Chan's eye. He was standing just behind the women, his face a blank slate, listening to them. Good man, Cole thought, and exhaled a controlled breath.

"You know-" Cole let his eyes settle back on Flynn. "It would go a long way if we knew your side of the story."

"What?" Flynn shifted to look at him.

"Why Hannah doesn't trust you."

"Didn't she tell you?"

"I want to hear your version," Cole reasoned, and internally he added, because Hannah doesn't remember.

"Well..."

Flynn blew out a breath and rested her hand on one hip. The way she cocked it to the side, Cole couldn't help but think of his mother and little sisters. They had all been so full of sass and independence and life... keyword there was *had*. They were all dead now.

"It's complicated," Flynn said finally.

"Try me," Cole countered.

"Well my boyfriend and I disagreed over whether to bring her. The vote had to be unanimous and I wouldn't say yes."

"Boyfriend?"

"Andy."

"Andy..." Cole narrowed his eyes. "Was *your* boyfriend."

"Yeah-"

Flynn had been about to answer. An explanation was spilling from her mouth, but that's when the fight started and all hell broke loose.

Lena was yelling, like actually yelling, and Cole turned just in time to see Hannah making a break for the tree line. He managed to blink maybe once before Chan was on her, wrapping his arms around Hannah's body and yanking her back.

"Shit," Cole spat and rounded the side of the cart with Flynn close on his heels.

A solitary scream erupted from Hannah's throat before Chan's hand clamped down over her mouth. The muffled cries continued while Lena jumped to her feet and flew at him. She was a wild thing, all black hair and scratching nails, beating her tiny fists on Chan's arms, shouting at him to let Hannah go.

Shit, shit, shit. Cole didn't feel like he was moving fast enough. All this noise was going to get them found.

Chan, for his part, stood resolutely still. He kept a tight hold on Hannah, whose eyes were wide and full of fear. But the beating he was taking from Lena was nothing short of impressive. Reaching up, she scratched at his face and he backed a step but didn't push her away, though his instinct was probably demanding he do so.

"What did you do to her?! What did you do?!" Lena shrieked the words until Cole looped an arm around her waist and dragged her back.

"Shhhh," he hissed in Lena's ear as he too placed a large hand over her mouth. This would definitely be a trigger for her, but there was just no way around it. They had to put an immediate stop to the noise. "No screaming, damn it. No screaming."

Flynn pulled up short, eyes darting between Chan and Cole, both of whom contained their still struggling victims with firm efficiency. The redhead for the briefest moment, was at a loss. Unusual for her, Cole figured. In his short experience thus far, she seemed to always have something to say.

"I will let you go," Cole whispered into Lena's ear, her whimpering was hard to take. "But you must promise not to yell. Understand?"

He could feel the tears leaking from her eyes now; they ran over his hand as it covered her mouth. Her breathing hitched, then hiccuped. She must be sobbing because she gave no response to his question.

Sucking in a breath, Cole locked eyes with Chan who was waiting for further instruction. Hannah's eyes were shut now, her body limp. Had she passed out again? Damn it.

"Nod your head, Lena," Cole spoke again, making an effort at being more gentle with his tone. "Promise me that you won't scream and I will let you go. Okay?"

"It's okay, Lena." Flynn held out her hands. "Nod your head sweetie and I'll get you."

Ten seconds passed, then twenty. Finally, Cole felt the most imperceptible of nods. Just like with a horse, once you feel them give you have to release immediately. Opening his arms, Cole let her go.

She staggered forward a few steps before collapsing into Flynn. They crumpled together on the barren ground, Flynn rocking slowly back and forth, stroking Lena's tangled black hair. Looking down on them, Cole had to dial back his guilt. He couldn't afford mistakes out here, it's what could cost you your life.

"What in the holy hell…" It was Liam, he was jogging into the clearing, the two horses trotting just behind. "Is going on here?"

"That's what I'm about to find out." Cole threw his answer over his shoulder before stepping up to Hannah.

Ducking his head, Cole peered into Hannah's face.

Chan removed his hand from her mouth and released her to step forward. Like Lena, she staggered once before falling into Cole's embrace.

He gathered her to him, kissing her hair and exhaling a shaky breath. How long would these episodes go on? His heart pounded and he wondered just how damaged Hannah really was. What the hell had happened to make her lose her memory in the first place? They needed answers, and fast.

"Well?" Cole raised his eyebrows at Chan who shifted to the side to make room for Liam.

"They were talking. A few names were mentioned," Chan explained. "Then Hannah bolted."

"Were they arguing?"

"No."

"Give me more."

"You want me to say the names?"

"What were they talking about? What do you think made her run?"

"They talked about the husband dying." Chan was careful not to say his name, it was clear he thought the names were the cause. "And another man was mentioned. They were supposed to meet with him."

Hannah tensed in his arms. She was listening, and maybe that was a good thing. Cole leaned back, trying to get a glimpse of her expression.

"He wasn't my husband," Hannah mumbled it, almost to herself.

"What?"

"He cut it out of me."

Hannah extended her right arm, her eyes bobbing from the scar on her trembling hand up to Cole, then back. Liam and Chan shared a glance, both of their brows furrowing.

"I'm remembering things." Hannah wiped at her mouth before closing her eyes. "Andy was not my husband. He was a friend… or he was supposed to be. I had a microchip in my hand, and my brother… Oh God, I was supposed to wait for him. He told me to wait for him."

Hannah's words caught in her throat and she began to cry. Cole placed a hand on the back of her head and pressed her face against his chest. This Andy asshole was getting mentioned more often these days and as far as Cole saw it, he was the pivotal cause for all of the suffering spread out around them.

Liam had told Cole the results of his interrogation. Slipping out of his bedroll to trade watch shifts one night, Liam spent a few extra minutes with Cole and they discussed the new developments. Good ole Andy, selling two women to get the items necessary to travel with a third. Part of Cole wished the guy wasn't already dead.

But now Hannah mentioned a microchip and a brother. There was so much going on behind that damn wall. Too much that Cole wasn't aware of, and it had to come to an end. He couldn't protect them all effectively if he was playing blind.

"Han-" Cole spoke the word quietly but looked straight at Liam as he talked. "Do you have all of your memories back, or are you just getting bits and pieces?"

"Just pieces and feelings. I'm sorry I ran. I had to get away."

"Liam," Cole said his friend's name and nothing more.

Maintaining eye contact, he communicated what they both already knew. It was time to get the full story from Flynn and Lena. They just couldn't afford to wait any longer.

"I know." Liam nodded and moved off.

Darkness was descending all around them and there was still so much that needed to be done. Glancing around, Cole caught the stares of Ace and Davey. They were standing in front of the cart, waiting, watching.

Extending a hand, Cole gestured for them both to get moving. There was firewood to collect, the mule to water, bedrolls to unload. Liam finished hobbling the gray horse beside a bucket filled with a minuscule handful of grain, then he threw a long leg over his bay and was off. With all of the screaming, he would have to make another quick sweep of the area, just to be safe.

"I'm sorry," Hannah spoke into Cole's chest. He could feel the movement of her lips against his shirt where the jacket lay open. "I didn't mean to freak out, but when the memories first come back it's like I'm living them. I'm in them."

"It's alright," Cole soothed her, running a hand up under her chin and tipping her face so he could look into her eyes. He didn't want to push her, didn't want to bring her pain, but he had lost a lot of ground by simply not asking her questions, and now it was putting everyone at risk.

"Can you tell me more? About the microchip? Your brother? What's behind the wall?"

That trusting face scrunched up and Hannah squeezed her eyes shut. Cole's heart stabbed at him in his chest, but he kept his breathing even, his face impassive. After a beat, she sucked in a breath and blinked up at him.

"I was inside the wall. It's metal and has cameras everywhere, but they were all off. I got the feeling Andy turned them off somehow but I don't know how. He was walking ahead of me. I wasn't supposed to be in there, but I felt like he could be for some reason."

Hannah glanced quickly over her shoulder at the two women still rocking on the ground a few feet away. She lowered her voice. Cole had to lean closer to hear her continue.

"I trusted him. Like he was my friend but that was all he was. Like I felt that was all he ever was to me. He knew my brother..." Hannah paused, swallowed, then seemed to force herself to continue. "Andy said my brother wanted him to bring me. But I knew that was all wrong because Uriah told me to wait for him. Then he was... he started to..."

"It's okay." Cole reached up and brought her face down against his chest again, ran a comforting hand through her hair. "That's enough. Thank you, I know that was hard."

Shifting his gaze up, Cole watched Ace and Davey build a fire. The twist of down branches they had collected from the forest floor were piled together with the two men hunched beside it. One was holding a homemade tinder bundle, and the was other striking his knife against the flint, throwing sparks. The wood was cold, but not overly wet so it should crackle to life given time and a fighting chance. They would all be warm tonight, maybe on the outside at least.

Eyes pivoting downward, Cole let his gaze flow over to Flynn. She was still cradling Lena, her arms wrapped protectively around the slight woman. But those hazel eyes were staring right into him. She had been watching first, and she did not look away.

Cole felt his jaw clench. There was no back down in that woman. Then again, there wasn't any in him either. She would give them what they needed… in the end.

THE SOUND OF HER SCREAMING, GOD IT FUCKING HURT HIM. Liam rubbed at his chest and pointed his bay horse back towards their makeshift camp. There was no one creeping around here, thankfully. No men had been drawn in by Hannah's cry.

Maybe they were just deep enough in the sticks now that she hadn't been heard, or maybe it was the dense fog all around them that suffocated most of the noise. Either way, it was black as pitch and twice as cold.

Why had Hannah lost it like that? Well, Liam could venture a pretty good guess. It was because of Flynn. He had turned his back on Hannah for just five damn minutes and that was all it took. This was his fault. But the horses had needed water and with Cole cornering the redhead, Liam figured she would be safe.

So, like an idiot Liam had walked away. He followed a low spot in the mountainside that eventually turned into a tiny creek. While he was kneeling down, filling his canteen Hannah's voice had erupted. One scream, all terror, then it was cut short.

The sick flood of adrenaline that had filled him made him angry, even now. He hated this... this weakness she brought out in him. The time it had taken for him to fling a leg over the nearest horse and hightail it back to camp was too long. The longest damn minute of his life.

And when he got there he had to dismount and be so quiet about it. You never knew what you were going to find. You couldn't just go charging in balls out. That was the thing. So he had to be so quiet on the outside when inside his head was blasting with noise.

Lifting his nose to the wind now, Liam inhaled. The scent of smoke curled on the air. The guys had gotten the fire going after all, that was good. It would make what he was about to do a bit easier.

There was nothing like the dance of flames to lull everyone into distraction. Watching the orange and red streaks move with that little blue center. Not to mention the warmth. The combination was mesmerizing. And it was just what Liam needed.

Shoving one hand into his jacket pocket, Liam eased the reins forward with the other until his bay was at a trot. Their twin breaths could be heard puffing as they climbed. The fire was just visible now through the thick trees.

Skirting the perimeter once, Liam pulled to a stop next to the gray horse and mule. The fire was situated as close to the cart as the team could manage without it catching from the flames. They wanted to get heat to Ryder but any attempt to move him might result in further injury so he had to remain lying down. The kid was even pissing in a canteen, which lovely Flynn had said was a good sign. Liam had to remind himself she was good for something.

Sometimes, while they all walked, Liam would hear the nurse murmuring to Ryder as the cart hitched and bumped along. She was good with him, truly, even Liam had to admit it. On one occasion, the kid had actually laughed. Well it was more of a laugh-cough then groan, which made Liam smile at first then frown. The kid had to make it... didn't he?

After tending to his horse, Liam stepped to the cart and peeked inside. Ryder was sleeping. The gentle rise and fall of the bedroll gave it away. Come on kid, Liam urged in his mind, before moving on to take a seat by the fire.

The team was spread out in a circle with Davey positioned closest to the cart, his back leaned against one wheel. Normally all of their sleeping bags would be lined up underneath it, but tonight they had a fire, so the bedding was currently being used as seating.

Hannah was tucked up beside Cole, as she had been this entire trip back. Despite Liam being in charge of her during the day, he kept his hands deliberately to himself. For the sake of appearances, Liam was just the bodyguard, stepping in to assist Cole who was so obviously busy.

Though the idea of giving up even the tiniest bit of his time with Hannah was difficult to swallow, both Liam and Cole had agreed that their little sharing arrangement was something best kept to themselves. They didn't know how Flynn and Lena would react and figured it would be best addressed once they all reached the safety of the compound. Plus, being with Hannah was admittedly a huge distraction and therefore a vulnerability.

And yes, Liam and Cole were working together like a well-oiled machine now. They were in crisis mode and years of training combined with a lifetime of friendship allowed them to slip easily into old roles. But this thing with Hannah was complicated and entirely too new. Liam wasn't quite sure how he felt about her going back to Cole and it was obvious the feeling was reciprocated.

But they had to put it aside. They'd table it and come back later, like they had a million other things in their past. When the time came to hash it all out? Well, Liam wasn't exactly sure of the outcome.

But for now it was all hands on deck and so he sat between Chan and Ace, directly across from Flynn who had a sleeping Lena snoozing on her lap. The team was crunching on some stale hard tac and Ace handed Liam a half eaten can of hot beans. The flames from the fire had burned off the label and the can was covered in black soot, but man they sure tasted good.

"Can't believe you saved me some," Liam commented, causing a chuckle to rise from the guys.

"Any sign?" Cole asked.

"None." Liam ducked his head and continued chewing.

The group dropped into silence, letting the crackle and pop of burning wood be the only sound. Liam knew what

Cole wanted, and he would get to it, he would. But there was something to be said of timing, and a feeling you got from years of asking questions.

Flynn needed to settle, she needed time to watch the flames dance. And so Liam finished his meager portion of beans and fished around in his bag for his ration of hard tac. Running low, everything was running low.

"Hmmm," Liam hummed, holding up the stale corn flour biscuit. "I think the last real meal I had was just before the war. It was that little hole in the wall place down on First Street. You remember it?" He gestured to Cole who smiled obligingly and nodded.

"Mama Le…" Cole lifted his eyes to the air, searching for the name. "Mama LeRoux's Cajun Kitchen."

"That's the one." Liam ducked his head, then crunched into the hard tac, speaking between bites. "Red beans and rice with that spicy sausage. Man, that was something."

"Yeah," Cole agreed, then looked to Ace and nodded.

"So, it was before the war-" Ace put his hands out about a foot from each other and grinned. "And the steak was this big, I swear it."

An indulgent chuckle spread around the fire as the rest of them chimed in. All the while, Liam kept Flynn in his periphery. He didn't look directly at her, but he watched for her reactions. Finally, the time came for her to share and he was not disappointed.

"Um, it was last year." She smiled at the memory, her hand stroking Lena's hair absently. "The RC just opened a second restaurant so my boyfriend took me. I had the veal piccata, it was to die for."

Silence. The guys felt the shock of what she'd just said like a kick straight to the gut.

Unlike when the others had shared, there was no laughter. No one smiled. No one nodded in agreement. But the mood had been so mellow before, so perfect, that it took Flynn several seconds to notice her mistake.

Here they all had been, for five long cruel ugly years, scraping by, barely surviving. Hell it was kill or be killed out here and she was eating at some new restaurant with her boyfriend. *New. Restaurant.* The words alone were enough to turn the stomach of any soldier.

But Liam was undaunted. He could roll with this, and it was perfect. Just fucking beautifully perfect.

As she glanced around, her face dropping at their expressions, Liam kept himself impassive and calm. He waited for her to rest her eyes on him; those intelligent, spitfire, hazel eyes.

Was it guilt he saw there? Pity? Fear? He didn't care, he could use them all.

"What's RC stand for?" Liam asked, his voice smooth, quiet.

"Um." Flynn hesitated, glancing at the ground a moment before sucking in a breath.

"We deserve to know," Liam stated. "We've been fighting for this country for the past five years, not to mention you in particular not a week ago."

"Refugee Center." Flynn tipped her head up, and locked eyes with Liam. "It stands for Refugee Center."

"It that what's behind the wall?" Liam asked.

"That *is* the Wall," Flynn corrected. "The whole complex, that's what we call it now… the Wall, because it surrounds everything."

"To keep the bad guys out?"

"That's what they told us." Flynn sighed, one hand stilled on the top of Lena's head. "In the beginning that's what it was for, I think. But now, it's to keep us in as much as anything else."

"Tell us about it," Liam prompted.

"I don't know where to begin."

"How did you get there?"

"She didn't tell you?" Flynn nodded at Hannah, and Liam knew it was time. He had to give if he was going to get.

"She doesn't remember," Liam admitted.

"Ah, the microchip. We always wondered what would happen if you removed it."

"You put it in her?"

"No." Flynn's face screwed up in disgust. "God no."

"You don't have one? And Lena?"

"No, we don't."

"Why not?" Liam pressed, and watched Flynn begin to squirm. Her face heated, she looked almost embarrassed. He better come back to it, he thought and threw her another question. "Do you have any marks on your back?"

"The barcode?" Flynn looked puzzled. "Yes, all genetically screened women got them. They were just getting around to processing the men when we left."

Liam's head was going about a million miles an hour. Questions pinged through his brain, fighting for priority. How many women? What's genetically screened mean? How many men are there? What's the age demographic? Who's doing this? Who's controlling this? What the hell is going on?

On the inside, he was a tornado, chaotic, fueled by outrage and anger. But on the outside, he was the picture of calculation.

Liam knew the worst thing he could do right now was let his questioning be ruled by emotion. It would get him nowhere. Well… at least nowhere he wanted to go.

So, purposefully he loosened the fingers of his right hand where it rested across his knee and dismissed the turmoil. When he clenched it back into a fist, his mind had snapped tight. Logic, order, tracking, proceed.

"How long have you lived inside the Wall?" Liam kept his gaze level.

"Um…" Flynn's face scrunched up with her thinking. "I'd say it was somewhere close to four years."

"How did you first come to be there?"

"They bussed us in, well some of us." Flynn hesitated before going on. "I mean, that's what you were asking right? Or?"

"Tell us your story Flynn." Liam leaned back ever so slightly. "We want to hear about you. Please."

Flynn gave a nervous laugh, the fire illuminating her

flushed cheeks. Glancing around, she eyed the people sitting so attentively all around her.

The men hadn't said anything, hadn't moved, hadn't hardly breathed since Liam started with his questions. For a moment, Liam himself even held his breath. Would she refuse? But then her eyes swiveled back to him and he saw the give there. And as soon as she sucked in a long breath, he released the one he'd been holding.

"It was about a year into the war," Flynn began. "I'm a nurse and the hospital that I was working at was exempt from the rolling blackouts. I remember that night clearly because I had been issued a pass to break curfew and there wasn't hardly anyone on the streets.

It was summertime so it had to be late. The city buildings were all dark and the stars were out, but it was warm. They weren't running busses anymore, no public transit anywhere, and the gas prices were so high. I couldn't afford to drive my car, so I walked."

Liam could picture it in his mind, what she said. The team had been knee deep in border skirmish shit by then. Cole's family was already dead and the bombs still rained down around them that summer.

Though it wouldn't be much longer before the fuel stores were attacked, drained and left to pollute the ground upon which they had sat. Then the flights stopped, and the tanks, and everything. But Flynn was a civilian, a nurse working at a hospital and she continued on with her story, unawares.

"My apartment was only a few blocks away but I never

made it there. I got a text message on my cell, which surprised me because the providers had all but collapsed at that point. The government did provide mobile charging stations and of course everyone made time for that because every few days the service would just pop to life and you could call your friends and family, make sure they were still alive.

So I get this text and it's a government alert, like a statewide thing, telling me to report to the local police station. I figure it's because I'm a nurse and maybe they know that or something and they need me. The station wasn't the easiest thing to find at first, but then there seemed to be more people walking all of a sudden, and I just followed them. I realized later it was everyone else who got that text."

Flynn paused and looked over at Hannah. Liam tensed, knowing she had something in particular to say, but he had to let this play out.

"You really don't remember any of this?" Flynn asked and Hannah just looked uncomfortable before pressing her face into the sleeve of Cole's jacket. After a beat, Flynn continued on.

"So once I got to the police station they processed us all in. There had to be over a thousand people there, I mean it was a lot of bodies. They searched us, took our phones and anything metal." Flynn huffed a laugh. "The crazy thing is, we all just did it. We all just went there, gave up our stuff and walked into those cells like a bunch of damn sheep. They told us it was for our safety. There was a chemical weapons threat and they were trying to contain it.

Some of the cells were bigger than others, there were more people in them but all of the space was used. It was standing room only. Even the benches had people standing on them because if you sat then someone would back into you and crush you. There was no extra room."

Flynn let her words die and glanced over again at Hannah who refused to meet her gaze. Liam sensed the story was stalling out, so after a second he interceded.

"Then what?"

"Well, I was lucky." Flynn's gaze popped back over to Liam. "They pulled out any and all 'skilled' workers first. They sorted us according to what we could do. Nurses, doctors, engineers, welders, mechanics. That's when I started to notice it. That's when it became more obvious."

"What?"

"There were no children. No one older than thirty-five, unless they were 'skilled.' And what was left standing in the cells?" Flynn made a face as if she had tasted something sour. "Women. Just women. At the time I felt afraid, just in that moment, but then I talked myself out of it. After all, most of the men in that age range were off fighting. Most had been drafted."

"The police did this?" Liam asked.

"Police?" Flynn snorted. "There were no more police, they had all been drafted. These were soldiers. These were North East Side Soldiers, our own soldiers. But they were just following orders. We were being moved to a refugee center for our own protection. Maybe they believed it, too. Maybe that's what it was originally designed for."

"But you don't think so," Liam supplied.

"No." Flynn shook her head, then a ripple of resolve passed over her face and Liam could tell he was losing her. The redhead shifted her body, causing Lena to stir, and locked eyes with Hannah. "Do you remember anything at all? Tell me what happened to Andy. Did you find Uriah?"

"We're asking the questions here." Liam's eyes darted between the women, noting how Hannah began to fold in on herself. "What's behind the Wall?"

"I told you, it's a refugee center."

"With restaurants? Where you lived for four years? Who runs it? Why did you all want to leave?"

"What side did you fight on?" Flynn let her eyes travel back to Liam, defiant, assessing.

"North East."

"If that's true then why didn't you come in with the rest of them? Why would they leave you out here?"

"Rest of who? North East Soldiers live inside the Wall?"

Flynn ducked her head and scooted out from under Lena causing the little dark-haired woman to wake. Groggily she rubbed at her eyes before Flynn stood and bent to pull Lena up by the arm.

Liam kept his gaze focused on the pair, all the while feeling the team tense. Holding his hand out flat, Liam signaled them all to settle without tipping Flynn off to his actions. She was shaking, trembling if he was being honest.

Whatever was going on with her, this shut down was

fueled by fear, not anything else. She was afraid of them. Afraid of what was behind that wall. Afraid.

"Look-" Flynn picked up the bedroll that Hannah had lent the women for the trip. "It's not that I don't appreciate what you guys have done for us, I do. Really I do. But unless you let me talk to Hannah, like really talk to her, then I can't say anything else."

"She doesn't have anything to say," Cole piped up, one hand wrapped protectively around Hannah, who kept her face averted.

"I'd like to be the judge of that." Flynn began shooing Lena towards the cart. "Because I'm not jeopardizing everything we've worked for on the word of a few Nor Side soldiers left out in the deadlands."

And with that the two women crawled beneath the cart and into their shared sleeping bag. Liam sucked in a breath and chanced a glance around. All eyes were on him and they all asked the same thing. What the *fuck* is going on?

THEY WERE HOME. THEY'D MADE IT. HANNAH COULDN'T believe the rush of relief that greeted her at the sight of the compound's gate.

There was still snow on the ground here, it lay in bunches beneath the trunks of trees and where the posts secured the gate to the ground. Anywhere the sun didn't often shine, the soft white substance had crystalized. But elsewhere, the dirt and brush mixed to reveal muddy patches of damp earth.

Hannah wanted to kneel down on it. She wanted to push her fingers into the icy soil, because here was safety. Here was stability and a chance to escape the tension that had plagued the group's every move for the past three days.

Ahead of her she heard Trey's shout, then Cookie's voice rising to match him. The two men were climbing the side of the cart, reaching their hands in towards Ryder.

Hannah's gut dropped then, she'd been so relieved to be here, she had almost forgotten the cost.

The fever had come on him yesterday, just when they'd all been thinking he was out of the woods. It burned bright and hot and fast. Flynn hadn't slept since. She stayed up all night and all day, drenching a torn up blanket with cold water from a canteen, pressing it along the back of Ryder's neck, around to his cheeks and forehead. His moans had continued to grow weaker and then he'd stopped eating altogether.

"We've got to get him to the stone house," Ace panted. He was equally drained, his face drawn with the stress of his dying friend. "He's dehydrated, and getting weaker. I need to grab the last of the penicillin from the storage cellar."

"I'll make a broth," Cookie announced, shooting a worried look at Trey who sniffed, scrubbing a hand roughly beneath his nose.

"What happened?" Trey whispered the question.

"He's been stabbed," Cole's voice was flat. "Now get some fresh bedding and set him up a bottom bunk in the stone house. We've got to make him as comfortable as possible. Get a fire going if there isn't one already."

Ryder let loose a pitiful cough. Hannah's face scrunched up and she looked at the ground. He had been suffering for so long it seemed. How was this fair?

"Now!" Cole barked and had everyone jumping.

Trey dropped back off the cart and stumbled a bit before he caught himself. Then he was running towards the stone house with Cookie jogging doggedly at his heels. Ace pulled on the mule and started the cart forward with Flynn bracing Ryder's body as it bumped through the narrow gate.

Abandoning his horse, Davey leapt up beside her and reached in to help hold his brother in place. Then Cole was dismounting, collecting Davey's reins and issuing orders. Hannah knew they were all overwhelmed. They were all tired and Cole was no exception. But he was like a freight train, he just wouldn't stop.

And so many things had to be done all at once. All the guys were needed to help carry Ryder from the cart into the bunk, even Cole. So Hannah walked up beside him as he addressed Liam and tugged the pair of reins from his hand. He whirled to look at her, his brow furrowed.

"I can take care of them," she said, and rolled her eyes at his disbelieving stare. "I've seen you both do it a thousand times, I can unsaddle them and turn them out to pasture."

Cole's eyes flicked to Lena who stood demurely beside Chan. He didn't trust her. Didn't want her to be left alone with Hannah. The dark-haired woman, still as dirty and disheveled as the day they'd found her, did not miss the implication of his glance.

"I'll stay with you," Lena offered Cole. "Or Liam, or Chan."

"Fine then," Cole replied. "Liam, she's in your line of sight at all times."

"Done." Liam nodded and then they were off.

Hannah only had time to watch the slightest of frowns

creep into Chan's face before he too headed for the stone house. Standing in place at the still open gate, Hannah watched them go.

Within a minute she was decidedly alone for the first time in over a week and the silence settled thickly into the air. It was only broken by the tired huff of horses beside her. Funny, the sound didn't strike fear in her heart the way it once had. In fact, she had come to absorb that sort of animal noise gratefully.

Turning back, Hannah walked a few steps to tug the heavy gate closed. She secured it with a metal chain before heading further into the compound. The horses followed willingly, heads low and swinging.

When they got to the storage building, the wooden door was hanging open, swaying slightly on its hinges. Hannah peeked her head inside, even called out, but it was empty. Ace must have come and gone. In his hurry he forgot to flip the latch to secure the door.

Hannah backed out and closed it, then moved on. She moved past Cole's cabin and the fire ring. Glancing up the hillside as she walked, Hannah could just make out the door to Liam's place. No one was there, of course. Everyone was at the stone house, helping Ryder.

Hannah wondered if they needed her too, but she couldn't really do anything special could she? She wasn't a nurse, or a medic. She wasn't even big enough to help hoist his body.

Shaking her head, Hannah felt even worse than useless, she felt helpless. Helpless to stop the death that was marching steadily towards the man who had become a trusted friend. Because that was what all of these men were to her now, she realized. They were her friends.

Pushing through the pasture gate, the horses began to nicker and paw at the ground. They were home, finally and that meant plentiful water, hay, and rest. Just inside the fence was a small shed where the saddles and other tack were stored. Hannah tied both horses up to a wooden post and went to work removing their burdens and cleaning them up a bit. Just down the rise, she spotted three shaggy white clouds munching along the picked-over ground. The sheep were unperturbed by the sudden reappearance of their much taller companions.

Finally done with the chore, Hannah released first the bay and then the gray to their freedom. After a few trotting steps, they both lay down in the dirt and rolled.

Taking a step back, Hannah leaned against the shed and watched. A sad sort of smile passed over her face. The animals rubbed and groaned, flinging their feet in the air and scooting all over the ground to itch themselves. After a minute, they both stood and shook vigorously, sending all sorts of dust and debris to fly in the air. Then off they went, down the hill, towards the fresh run of water and the sparse grass.

"Hey," Liam's voice broke the scene as he pushed his way into the pasture, dragging the mule behind him.

"Hi." Hannah brightened when she saw him, taking a step closer, but then his mouth puckered and he gave a quick shake of his head. He didn't want her approaching him.

After a beat Hannah saw why. Little Lena still trailed him, and her quiet eyes were watching their interaction. Inside, Hannah's heart deflated a bit. Ever since the raid, Liam had kept her at arm's length. He protected her yes, but that was the extent of it. There was no sharing his sleeping bag, no holding her hand or sneaking a kiss when no one was looking. She had said no public affection before, but he seemed to be taking it to another level.

"I just need to take care of the mule and then we've got to haul fresh water up to the stone house," Liam explained. Hannah nibbled at her lip. Maybe he was just upset about Ryder, and after things settled down they'd have a chance to reconnect.

"Can I help?" Hannah asked.

"Um," Liam considered, brushing with firm strokes all along the animal's back and shoulders. "Sure, you could get some of the buckets from my cabin and Cole's. We need to clean him up, and I was thinking Lena and Flynn, eventually, would like to wash, too. Maybe we could heat up some water to make it more tolerable."

"They could use the tub in Cole's cabin," Hannah suggested. "It's not very big, but it's better than a sponge bath."

"I have to watch her every second," Liam reminded her, one eyebrow cocked.

"That's alright." Lena was quick to jump in, taking a step closer. "You can keep your back to me."

"Huh." Liam pressed his lips together and continued working at the mule, bending low to pick out his hooves. All the while, the two women watched him. Hannah felt a strange sort of concern but then he righted himself and nodded his head. "Okay, but I won't have time for it for a few hours more."

"Thank you." Lena's pale cheeks flushed before she glanced down. Hannah nibbled at her lip and looked away.

"Well, I'll get a fire going to heat it and haul some fresh water from the stream," Hannah managed finally. "Do you need buckets for Ryder first?"

"No." Liam shook his head and turned the mule loose. "We'll haul the water for Ryder and you just focus on the bath thing for the girls."

"Okay." Hannah let her hands come together in front of her body, one finger twisting in her other hand's grasp.

Stepping forward she chanced another look at Liam, but he was already turning away. In a few giant strides, he was back through the pasture gate with Lena close on his heels. He didn't throw Hannah so much as a backwards glance.

Letting loose a long sigh, Hannah contemplated. What was this strange sort of trepidation she felt? She hoped it wasn't some kind of forewarning about what would become of Ryder. No, that couldn't be it. He was tough, like Ace had said. He would survive. Hannah was just tired, she told herself, all of them were.

But being tired didn't change the task at hand and Hannah was determined to make herself useful in any way possible. So she returned to Cole's cabin, started a fire and carried two empty wooden buckets down to the stream.

Then she hauled them back up the hillside, stopping every so often to put them down and heave in a few breaths. Why was water so heavy? But eventually she made it back to the fireplace and set them on the grate to warm.

Standing back a moment, Hannah swiped her hand across her sweating brow. She shrugged out of her jacket and sat on the edge of the narrow bed. Unlacing her boots, she kicked them off with a groan. They would need more firewood from the pile outside but she just had to rest her feet a second. Then there was the fact that it was getting darker already. The days didn't last as long this far into winter.

With a sigh, she pushed off the bed and crossed to the dresser. Cole kept a few candles inside the top drawer. When she slid it open, she ran her hands over his carefully folded clean clothes.

There were a few plaid button down shirts and several solid colored cotton t's. For the sake of traveling light, the team had only been allowed one change of clothes each during their journey. Longingly, Hannah glanced over her shoulder at the buckets of water being warmed by the fire. She wished the bath was for her, but knew the other women needed it more.

With another sigh, she let her eyes travel back to the dresser and she fished out two homemade candles. Taking them over to the fire, she lit the wicks and then set them each in a metal holder, one on a shelf just beside the tub and the other back on the dresser. If she couldn't bathe, Hannah thought, then at least she could change into fresh clothes.

Humming to herself, she unbuttoned her jeans and stepped out of them. They were one of two pair she had worn in order to keep warm and also attempt to disguise the swell in her hips that marked her as female from a distance. She shimmied out of the second pair and pulled off her socks along with them.

All of these things would need a good wash. There was still dried blood from Ryder splattered everywhere. The thought made her heart squeeze tight and she had just sucked in a breath when the front door slid open.

Turning her head, Hannah looked over her shoulder, her hands pausing at the hem of her shirt.

"Don't stop on my account." Cole's voice was gravely and low as he entered, shifting the mood in the small space.

Hannah watched him let loose a small breath before turning away from her to shut the front door. When he looked back, he had a familiar look on his rugged face. He wanted to watch her undress. He liked that, she knew. His green eyes deepened in their intensity as he stared at her and it caused Hannah's blood to heat in response.

Clearing her throat she glanced down at her hands, still clutching the bottom of her navy-blue shirt. Well, really it was his navy-blue shirt, cut down to her size. Up and over her head it went. Hannah released the clothing to fall down to the wooden floor but she kept her gaze ahead of her, on the wall.

"How's Ryder?" She asked, she could hear Cole stalking towards her.

"Still alive," Cole whispered. "But I can't talk about it anymore. Please, let's not talk about it right now, okay?"

"Okay."

Hannah exhaled as Cole stepped up behind her, wrapping his arms around her body and pulling her in against him. She felt his lips press gently against her spine. The tickle of his short beard moving along her bare skin sent a spattering of goosebumps to travel down her arms.

"I love you," Cole said the words between slow kisses. His mouth traveled up to the back of her neck, then along her shoulder. "Have I told you that lately? That I love you?"

"Mmmm," Hannah hummed a response, her body warming and relaxing at his contact. "Not lately, no."

"Well I do, woman," Cole persisted, and his arms clutched her body tighter, pressing the length of his body along hers. "And I worry about you, and what's going on in that head of yours."

Hannah stiffened a moment but Cole did not relax his grip. If anything he held on tighter. Tilting her face to the side, she eyed him out of her periphery.

"Let's not talk about it right now, okay?" She echoed his words from earlier and he gave her a slight nod.

"So I guess talking is off the table then," Cole teased.

Slipping his rough fingers into the seam of her underwear, he pushed them slowly down off her hips. Hannah's insides ached and her pulse quickened as he continued to guide them down her thighs, he even crouched to drop them past her knees.

When they landed on the floor he looked up at her, a sly smile touching the features of his face. Hannah's eyes grew wide as Cole began steadily kissing his way back up her body. He took his time about it until he had returned to standing just behind her.

His hands stroked along her chest, cupping her breasts before gliding down to her tummy and lower. The little gasp that escaped her mouth had him nipping at her shoulder and before long he was tugging out of his jeans and flinging off his shirt.

Arching her back, Hannah shifted her hips against him until he let out a groan that had her yearning for more. She loved the way he sounded when he really wanted her. It did something to her, sent a thrill of power surging through her bloodstream.

His fingers tensed on her waist. He pressed in closer. Rotating her around to face him, Cole slid his hands beneath her butt and in one effortless move lifted her to sit on the dresser. His lips found hers then, turning their drawn out contact into one of hot sparking demand.

He was always like this. Though he made every effort at being slow, Cole's lovemaking always ended in blazing passion. And Hannah loved that about him. Loved what he did to her, loved what she made him powerless to stop.

So she reached between them and took him in her hand, guiding him inside of her. He hissed out a breath into her mouth and she knew this hadn't been his plan, but she was more than ready for him. Once inside her, he couldn't help himself.

Wrapping her legs around his waist, she moved her body in time with his. A low groan worked its way from his throat and he buried his face in her neck, sucking and licking at her skin. She threw her head back and closed her eyes, absorbing the sensations he created inside her.

The friction between them only intensified until she was biting her lip and squeezing her eyes shut, fighting against the tide that threatened to overtake her. But there was no use, because his hands shot to her hips and he was calling her name and in the moment that he released, he took her over the edge with him.

She cried out, her body tightening around him, the whole world going white. When she felt herself start to float back, all she heard was the sound of his panting before she felt the gentle brush of his lips beneath her chin. She loved this man, really she did. And she would do anything to keep him.

"Are you sure you don't want to clean up?" Liam asked.

"No, I'm fine." Flynn waved him away.

Frowning, Liam stood, arms folded over his chest, leaning against the bunk bed where Ryder lay sleeping. Finally sleeping. Not moaning or thrashing or gasping for air, as he had been when they first moved him. It was torture.

Liam's eyes shifted away from the determined redhead kneeling on the floor and over to Davey. He was sitting on a far bunk, his head cradled in his hands, sobbing. The little dark-haired girl patted tentatively at his back. Liam's brow furrowed further, if that was possible.

Even now, with Davey so obviously crumbling before her, it was hard for Lena to touch him. Though she wanted to offer comfort, it was like the moment her hand skimmed the back of his shirt, she sucked back as if she'd been burnt.

It was so familiar. Everything she did was so painfully familiar. What a miserable shit show, Liam thought, and let loose a sigh.

"Ace can watch him for an hour or two while you wash," he reasoned.

He wasn't sure why he felt so persistent about the subject. It was just that the two women hadn't been given the chance to bathe yet. The streams were icy cold on their trek back, and the team hadn't wanted to stop during the day and waste precious time.

Sure, Flynn had scrubbed at her hands and forearms the second they had reached the stone house, but the rest of her was a mess.

"You mean *that* guy?" Flynn tossed her head towards the bunk above Davey.

Ace's arm hung limp over the edge of the bed. His heavy breathing could be heard making quiet ripples throughout the room. The medic had walked the entire way home while Flynn had ridden in the cart, so Ace was out cold. Not to mention that neither of them had slept much since Ryder came down with the fever.

Liam huffed out a breath and let his eyes fall back over to Ryder. He only hoped that the injection Ace gave the kid would work. That, and the rich broth Cookie had made him; although halfway through the bowl, Ryder had dropped off into sleep. Flynn had been spoon-feeding him while he lay on his belly.

"You can't go on this way," Liam cautioned and caught a haughty glare from Flynn.

"What do you care?" She spat.

"Fine." Liam rolled his eyes before gesturing to Lena. "You still up for it?"

The little porcelain girl-doll shoved to her feet and pattered quickly his way. She didn't say anything, keeping her face downcast and her hands tucked behind her back. A sudden flash of anger wanted to consume him at her meekness but he dialed it back. The assholes responsible were all dead. You couldn't kill a man twice, though Liam himself had imagined it almost constantly with his own father, so there was that.

Rolling his shoulders, Liam waited for Lena to come alongside him before turning his back on Flynn and striding into the main living area of the stone house. When he had first been given the assignment to watch her, he'd been annoyed. He had other things to do aside from babysit. Plus, though she was quiet, the girl was also intelligent and actually quite lethal, if you gave her a knife and showed her where to put it.

But between carrying Ryder into the house, unloading the cart, prepping the mule and hauling water, Lena had stayed within his line of sight the entire time. She hadn't darted away or made a move for a weapon. She made his job easy, staying close and yet not underfoot.

For the most part, she remained silent, which suited Liam just fine. Though he didn't want to admit it, he was pretty damn tired himself. And the mind fuck that Flynn had unleashed on them all hadn't helped either. Thankfully, Trey and Cookie had offered to take over all watch shifts for twenty-four hours so that meant the majority of them could sleep straight through.

Of course that didn't answer the question of where Lena and Flynn would be sleeping tonight or what the protocol was going to be moving forward with them. But that was part of Cole's job. His circus, his monkeys. Liam huffed a breath.

Twisting his neck to one side in an attempt to stretch out the tension, he cruised through the warmth of the living area and out into the night. The darkness and wind greeted them as they breached the door. Lena, as always, kept close on his heels.

As they slipped and slid a bit down the rocky slope towards Cole's cabin, Liam thought absently about making some sort of permanent path. They could build a tiered stair system of sorts using cut logs. It would certainly make things easier now that the stone house was their main meeting area. Everyone trying to traverse the slope was wearing down the dirt, making it too loose in some places.

When they reached Cole's door, the place looked dark but then again his lone window was on the far side of the cabin. Liam glanced at Lena who came to a stop next to him before knocking on the solid wood door. He used to spend quite a bit of time with Cole here, hanging out, working on stuff together. But ever since Hannah came around, the space had been off limits.

Rolling his shoulders again, Liam worked to ease the

tightness in his jaw at the thought of her just inside. But then the door pulled open and he lost the fight, his teeth clenching all the more.

"Hey." Cole was tucking in his shirt, his pants unzipped, his hair all a mess. "The bath right?"

"Right," Liam managed.

His eyes darted over Cole's shoulder to where Hannah smoothed at her golden locks. She was already dressed in fresh clothes, thankfully, but the flush in her cheeks was a familiar one.

Liam's gut churned, but he couldn't look away. He knew she belonged to Cole, too. That was how this thing was supposed to work. In fact, she had been Cole's for a few months before Liam was added to the mix and that hadn't bothered him before. But for some reason, being here now with the two of them, it made his blood simmer.

This is your best friend and the woman you... like. This is what you've all agreed to. The thoughts played quickly though his head. He didn't like the anger that brewed inside of him, so he battled against it.

"Come on in." Cole stepped to one side while he fastened his pants and ran a quick hand through his hair. "There are another few candles in the dresser you can light and Hannah laid out a change of clothes that might fit Lena."

"Alright." Liam cleared his throat before focusing on the clothes set neatly on the bed. An idea came to him. After all, you got more flies with honey than vinegar. "Do you have any that would fit Flynn? She won't leave Ryder to wash, but maybe some fresh clothes would be a good compromise."

"I do," Hannah replied.

She gave Liam a small smile before turning to rummage through the dresser against the far wall. When she straightened, she held up a button down shirt, pair of jeans and clean socks.

"They're my last pair but maybe I could work on making some more," Hannah added.

Her easy manner had Liam softening and as she brushed past him he was tempted to reach out and grab her hand. But then Lena stepped into his line of sight and he remembered why he had to hold back.

Reluctantly, Liam kept his fist at his side, only allowing himself a glance over his shoulder as Hannah headed out into the night. Cole held the door for her as she exited and gave Liam a little nod before shutting it.

For a beat, Liam let himself be swallowed by his inner turmoil. Then the little dark-haired girl shifted, bringing him back to the present once more. Purposefully, he cleared his mind.

"Sure you're comfortable with this?" Liam asked.

"Hannah said you don't hurt women," Lena offered, her eyes falling to the buckets of steaming water half pulled back from the fire.

"That's still true, at least," Liam agreed.

Removing his jacket, he tossed it on the bed and moved to pour the first bucket into the carved out wooden tub. It was small, way too small for a man, but Lena would probably fit just right. The water swirled and filled the smoothed out bottom.

Absently he wondered if it wouldn't be too hot. He may need to grab a cold water bucket from the corner. While he worked, Lena crossed to the small dresser and moved to light the other candles using coals from the fire. It could use another log or two, now that Liam thought of it.

"You'll turn your back?" Lena asked, coming up beside him to look down at the tub.

"I will but…" Liam hesitated, knowing what he had promised.

"But what?"

"But I have a hard time keeping my back to anyone," Liam admitted. "Even tiny girls with no weapon."

"Okay…" Lena exhaled a shaky breath and they stood in silence together. "What if you turn your back while I get in, then I'll be the one to face away from you. You stay on the bed, though, you don't get off that bed."

"I can do that." Liam nodded, as guilt swamped him.

Of course Lena would feel better with a woman watching her, but Hannah couldn't be left alone with her or Flynn. And Cole was right to have both new women monitored for the first several weeks.

The team still didn't know what was behind that wall, or what was really going on. So despite the fact that Lena didn't seem like a threat, they had to take every precaution. At least at first.

"Just…" Lena sucked in a breath. "Promise me."

"I promise." Liam looked down into her eyes, suddenly

filled with trepidation. "I swear I won't move from the bed."

Exhaling, Lena just nodded while Liam backed to the mattress and turned away from her. Behind him, he listened to her movements. Closing his eyes, he let his senses monitor her progress. Her clothes rustled, then dropped one by one onto the swept wooden floor. Then there was the trickle of water, a hiss of breath.

"Too hot?" Liam asked.

"No." Lena let out a tiny gasp. "No, it's good."

Water rippled and lapped at the wooden sides of the tub and he heard her let out another hiss as she sank inside. There should be a bar of soap nearby, but he didn't check, keeping his back to her as promised.

"Okay," Lena said finally. "You can turn around."

Crawling further up onto the bed, Liam shifted to sit with his back up against the wall so he could see Lena. Her dark hair was wet now and as he watched, she splashed more water onto her head using her hands. Reaching for the tiny shelf that ran along the wall, Lena grabbed the bar of soap before sparing him a quick glance over her shoulder.

For several minutes, they settled into silence.

Lena scrubbed at her face, then moved to her shoulders and down her arms. In the dim light from the fire and flickering candles, he could see the array of bruises that mottled her body. It was a sickening sight to him, way too reminiscent of his childhood, so he swallowed and looked away.

"I never thanked you," Lena spoke. Her voice was tiny, like she was.

"I'm sorry we didn't find you sooner," Liam answered, his eyes returning to her back, and the code that was printed there.

"Not just for the rescue part," she confided, hesitating in her washing. "For the... for the..."

"Killing part?" Liam supplied.

He knew what she meant. She wanted to thank him for the opportunity to slit that fucker's throat. But no matter how much that bastard had deserved it, the act itself would likely haunt Lena forever. Taking life was not easy, though the team seemed to think it was easy for Liam. Maybe he was just too good at making it look like that, and of course, some kills were way easier than others.

"Yeah," Lena answered, then cleared her throat. "Does it ever... I mean, does the..."

"No." Liam shook his head. "It never goes away, you'll always see him. I'm sorry, maybe I should have mentioned that."

"That's okay," Lena rushed to answer, giving him another look over her shoulder. "I would have done it anyway."

Liam nodded in understanding and they both fell back into silence. She leaned forward and washed her legs and feet, then reached up to lather her hair. After rinsing completely, she sank down and let her legs dangle over the edge of the tub. He heard her sigh, and it released a tension that Liam hadn't known his own body was carrying.

"I wasn't bussed to the refugee center, not like Hannah and Flynn," Lena supplied, though she kept her face averted, speaking to the wall. "I arrived much later, maybe even in the last shipment. We were packed into train cars. Not the nice kind with seats, but the ones used to carry boxes and stuff. It wasn't super crowded though, I slept most of the way."

Why are you telling me this? Liam felt the question on the tip of his tongue, but he held himself back. Sometimes all it took was one misplaced interjection to ruin the flow of a confession. He had done so on more than one occasion in the past, mostly when he had first begun learning the art of interrogation.

But he was a quick study and soon after those experiences he learned to pace himself. It was all in the timing. So he kept his breath even and quiet, waiting for Lena to decide how much she would give him. And he wanted to hear it all, every little detail.

"I'm from Kentucky, so we were right on the border when the war first broke." Lena brushed the surface of the water with one hand while she spoke, as if she could see her hometown in front of her. "It was weird right? How the line split diagonally across the country like that. Like the big Carolina military bases were pit against the big California military bases until they basically destroyed each other. I always wondered about it, maybe I'm the only one."

"No, it was weird," Liam agreed and watched her hand still a moment, but then she just nodded.

"Do you know what it was about? The fighting?"

"I don't."

"Well, I guess it doesn't matter now." Lena shifted to tuck both her legs back into the tub a moment, hugging her knees to her chest.

"What was it like?" Liam asked the open-ended question, hoping to stir another detailed response.

"When I first saw the Wall it was shining so bright in my eyes, I kept blinking and blinking. After a few nights closed up in the train car, the reflecting sunshine was painful." Lena leaned back once more, relaxing into her story. "The tracks went right up to it, then ended at the wall itself.

And man is that thing high, maybe two hundred feet? A twenty story building? I don't know. But the soldiers unloaded us and then we all walked through using a metal door. It was no bigger than the door on this cabin.

Once we made it all the way through, it was like walking into the past. There were beautiful paths lined with trees and grass, brand new apartments, office buildings, parks, and it all had power. The noise was insane.

There were people everywhere, walking, jogging, riding bicycles and electric scooters. I just dropped to my knees right there, you know? I had seen everyone I care about die, everything I grew up with burn, and here was this safe haven all along. I was so angry at first, but then so relieved."

Lena dropped into silence and for several seconds, Liam watched her. She lifted a trembling hand to her face, wiped at her eyes and sniffed. It didn't take a rocket scientist to tell she was crying, but she was so very quiet about it.

Remaining on the bed, Liam gave her time to compose herself, but when her hand returned to the water, she didn't go on. Finally, he decided it was time to pursue.

"How long did you live there?"

"Um." Lena cleared her throat. "Around three years I think."

"What was it like?"

"It was like living in any city, but a very tightly controlled one." Lena looked up at the ceiling, as if thinking a moment. "There were tens of thousands of people there, like you could fill a stadium with them. But right away you could see how the women outnumbered the men, like by a lot. And there weren't any kids… also not many people over the age of forty, and those that were had a profession from before."

Why? Liam was dying to ask but he knew that question was a loaded one and it may cause her to shut down. *Patience buddy.*

"I was placed in a small apartment with Hannah and Flynn. It was a pretty nice three bedroom despite the size, with one full bath and a living room. There wasn't any kitchen, though. None of the homes had kitchens. You had to eat at one of the two food courts, or later, at the restaurant."

"Was the food any good?" Liam asked, and knew he'd hit the mark when Lena huffed a laugh.

"Yeah, actually it wasn't so bad. But they regulated everyone's portions and it was super super healthy stuff."

"So no ice cream."

"No ice cream."

Silence. Lena glanced around then, her eyes catching on a towel folded neatly on the floor at her side. Uh-oh, Liam realized, he was losing her.

"Is that why you left?" Liam jumped in with both feet, his time was up, better make it count. "The portion control and lack of ice cream?"

"No." Lena shook her head, and her hands began to tremble once more.

"Did they hurt you? Force you to do anything?"

"Not exactly… it's complicated." Lena rose quickly, revealing the back of her nude body for a split second before grabbing for the towel and wrapping it around her.

"I can't tell you certain things." Lena turned to face him, her eyes were a mix of pleading and fear. "Please turn around while I dress."

"Because Flynn told you that you couldn't?" Liam asked, before shifting to face the wall once more.

"Yes, but I also don't want to screw everything up. It could be our only chance."

"Only chance at what?"

"Of taking down the Wall."

Breakfast was good. The hot cornflour pancakes were drizzled in melted butter, like the most delicious butter Cole had ever tasted. While most of the team had been away, the goat milk had managed to stack up, so Cookie had taken the time to make a sort of creamy spread *and* butter.

It was enough to make Cole consider smiling, but not enough to actually do it. At least not until Liam plunked down in the chair across from him and began to murmur his news. Lena was talking. Not a lot of talking, but enough.

Given time, Cole figured that she'd probably tell Liam a great deal more. This was just the break they needed since Flynn was as tight-lipped as she was hard-assed. Though admittedly her resolve impressed him. The fiery redhead was actually snoring in the bunk room just next door at this very moment.

Cole shook his head, battling a blend of frustration and appreciation. She was withholding valuable information, potentially putting them all at great risk. But at the same time her single-minded devotion to Ryder's care was beyond admirable. Even Ace admitted he wouldn't have been able to keep Ryder alive this long without her. She was a tornado force wind, one blowing in all directions, that was for sure.

"Well don't thank me all at once ya bunch a heathens," Cookie spat, as he set down a full plate in front of Liam.

"Thanks, Cook," Cole chimed, but Liam only grunted.

The older man grumbled under his breath before moving back towards the fireplace and the sizzling food he had cooking there. Hannah's slender frame bent to help him and had Cole staring just a moment longer, appreciating the weight she had gained and the places it filled out.

He felt his body stir at the memory of last night and gave his head a purposeful shake to clear it. There was too much work to be done to lose focus. Trey was currently on watch duty, Ace was monitoring Ryder, and Davey was passed out in the bunk room, too. It was a good thing they had waited those two weeks before executing the mission or else all of this much needed space would not have been usable when they returned.

Keeping Ryder alive involved more than just good meds and a prayer. It was a warm room, dry bedding, fresh water, rich food and constant monitoring. Stone house made all of those things possible now that it was complete.

Cole was grateful to be proved right, though the circumstances sucked big time.

"Hey," Chan muttered as he took a seat next to Liam. Was no one in this crew a morning person?

"Good morning." Cole surveyed the two lumps hunched before him. "We need to start rotating in on the watch again, but I don't think Davey is up for it. Too much silent time spent thinking."

Chan and Liam just blinked down at their plates, stabbing at the hotcakes and bits of meat gratefully. It wasn't bacon. Cole couldn't remember the last time he had indulged in such a luxury as pig meat, but it was protein and not so terribly dry when you mixed it in with the butter.

There had been talk last summer of hogs being spotted southwest of here, but the team had never been able to agree on sending a hunting party out. Could be too much of an unnecessary risk, considering they had the sheep producing right here.

"I was thinking Davey could start in on the more labor intensive stuff, haul wood and water, that kind of thing," Cole supplied.

Still no response from the men before him. "That would put Chan up for the first watch shift after Trey and then I'll go," Cole tried again.

"What about me?" Liam asked, giving the first real sign he had been listening.

"Well, you've got your assignment already. Babysit Lena, get more intel."

"What? Come on," Liam protested, which came as a surprise to Cole, he rarely disagreed. "I can't keep watching her all day and all night. Put someone else on it. Chan can do it."

"I'll do it," Chan was quick to agree, his brown eyes snapping up at the same time his fork landed squarely on the table.

"You already have a rapport built with her, Lee." Cole narrowed his eyes. "You're the expert here, we need this info."

"Stone house is too crowded already," Liam persisted. "I can't continue sleeping here just to keep an eye on her. Let whoever is monitoring Ryder watch her at night."

"So bring her to your cabin," Cole reasoned. "Let her sleep there."

"You've got to be kidding me," Liam hissed.

"What?" Cole put his hands out in supplication, wondering at the two men glaring at him from across the table.

"Unbelievable," Chan muttered.

"Look-" Cole lowered his voice. "You got her to open up last night in the bath. You can do it again."

"You *watched* her bathe?" Chan was incredulous. "How could you do that? Don't you get what she's been through?"

"Easy tiger." Liam shifted to look at Chan. "I stayed across the room and she had her back to me the whole time. By the way, she does have the marks, too. Maybe one of you guys should look at them."

"That's a good idea," Cole agreed. Leaning forward, he

rubbed absently at his beard, it could use a trim. "Do you think you could just outright ask her, or…?"

"I don't know," Liam's words dripped with sarcasm as he shoved back from the table and stood up. "I guess I'll find out during my *babysitting* gig."

What the…? Cole let his mouth drop just a fraction as he tilted back in his chair and watched Liam's progress. The tall fucker was extra grumpy as he stomped into the bunk room and retrieved Lena.

She didn't look all that bothered by the arrangement though as she came scampering after him towards the far door, tucking her shining black hair behind one ear. Cole heard Liam grumble about checking on the livestock before he plowed through the door and into the daylight.

Hannah peeked at Liam over her shoulder as he left, but said nothing.

"I want to see the code in person," Chan said, breaking into Cole's train of thought.

"Oh. Yeah, of course."

"Make sure to let me know *before* you have her take her clothes off for you." Chan's voice was tight and his face unusually expressive. He was pissed, too.

"Jeez, Chan chill out." Cole rolled his eyes and pushed back from the table. "I'll let you know."

After a terse nod from Chan, Cole cleared his plate and dropped it by Hannah. His two most stoic guys were considerably off their game today. It threw Cole for a bit of a loop, but in true fashion he shoved it aside. Let them be bitchy, that's okay. He would just keep powering through for the sake of the team… like always.

With everyone occupied, Cole left the stone house and pointed his boots towards the top of their property. The fence wasn't all that far and once he got to it, he followed its line through the thick trees and underbrush.

It was cold, with snowy patches still on the ground in the shady areas. As he hiked, he kept his eyes fastened on the fence, checking for weak spots. When he found one, he stopped and glanced around, then dragged some freshly downed branches to wedge and brace in the low spot.

Before too long, he arrived at the tree stand where Trey was hidden. Looking up at the gnarled oak, Cole could just make out the flash of auburn hair that creeped out from beneath Trey's hat. If he hadn't known where to look though, he never would have seen him.

Cole let loose a low whistle and stepped clear just in time to miss the rope ladder as it unfurled to the ground. They'd built the wooden platform in the tree practically the first day they'd arrived. From its position, you could see all the way around the compound. There were only a few blind spots, and those were fortified with extra high sections of fence.

Hooking his hands and feet in the sagging rungs of the ladder, Cole climbed steadily, his breath puffing as he went. By the time he reached the platform, Trey offered him a hand and pulled him through the narrow hole just wide enough to fit a man's body.

"What brings you up?" Trey asked, dusting off his hands and stepping aside to give Cole some room.

"Just an update in the schedule."

Taking two steps, Cole walked to the railing and looked out. It was breathtaking up here. The clouds swirled in the sky, with beams of light bursting through every so often to shine down on the earth. Rotating around, Cole surveyed the array of smoke that flumed up in pillars further out.

There were many more groups living in that direction, in the low lands, or as Flynn called it, the deadlands. It had been a while since any of them had made contact, which was good in a way and bad in another. The good was none of the others dared enter the team's territory. The bad was that the longer the team stayed away, the more suspicious the others would get.

If you didn't make your presence known every few months, or at least once a season, then rumors began to spread. And with rumors, curious minds, and with curious minds then eventually visitors. They could not risk any visitors. They could not risk someone coming along and discovering the women here. It would be the end for all of them if word like that got out.

"Been quiet," Trey remarked.

His hands were stuffed into the pockets of the watch coat. Though the platform had a roof, it was entirely open to the wind and therefore extremely cold during winter. The team only had one trench coat between them and so had lined it with sheep skin for extra warmth. The coat stayed up here and was traded back and forth between men for the watch. It made the task doable if not enjoyable.

"Too quiet?" Cole asked.

"Yeah, but everyone else is staying put." Trey gestured to the fires. They knew where each one came from and took note if one failed to burn for more than a few days at a time. "That we know about, of course."

"Of course," Cole echoed him, then fell silent, contemplating.

Might be time for a run into the fallen city, get their faces out there, trade a few things, hustle back. It was something to consider, that was for sure, but Cole had a lot of things to think about these days so he put it on the bottom of his mental list.

"So, what's the schedule change, boss?" Trey prompted, he never did like to stay quiet for long.

"Chan's going to come up in a bit and stay through dinner. I'll relieve him and stay a full night, and then you can come back at dawn. Eventually we'll rotate Cookie in for some relief but that will be it for a while. At least until we know whether Ryder's going to pull through."

"Got it." Trey paled considerably. "How's he doing?"

"He's breathing," Cole answered, then added. "Ace says it will take a week before we can tell if the penicillin worked or not. If it did, then he's got a good chance. If not..."

"He will." Trey tipped his chin up. "He'll make it."

THE LIGHT FROM THE CRESCENT MOON TRICKLED IN through the window above the bed. Hannah rolled onto her side and let her fingertips tap at the icy pane. Cole's cabin was warm enough, though the fire was burning low. He had been working the night watch for almost a week now, so she had extra time to herself. Time to think, and stretch out on the narrow mattress. Some of that was good, and maybe some wasn't so good.

Blowing out a slow breath, Hannah gathered her hand back to her body and burrowed further under the heavy covers. She blinked at the shifting clouds that passed steadily over the darkened sky, obscuring the stars and the moon alike. Ryder was holding tough. Two days ago he started talking more and just yesterday he actually sat up.

It was only for a few seconds, but still, a really great sign. Or so Flynn had said. She hadn't spoken directly to Hannah, of course, but to the room in general when it had happened. And the look of relief on Davey's ashen face had been so beautiful, it made Hannah want to cry. But there could be no crying in front of Flynn.

Hannah still didn't have any specific memories of the other woman, and the idea that Andy had been Flynn's boyfriend was a bit sickening to be honest. The information only made Hannah all the more reluctant to speak directly to her. How would she explain Andy's insistence that they had been married?

Thankfully Flynn no longer tried, which made things easier. The redhead ignored Hannah completely, which felt absolutely right if Hannah was being honest. That was typical for them. She felt it somewhere deep down, Flynn pretending like Hannah didn't exist. And that was okay by her, really okay.

But then there was Lena. She constantly followed Liam around, helping him with every little task. She was never far from his side, and when she wasn't beside him, her eyes tracked his movements. It was frustrating. Hannah had tried to approach Liam on several occasions, but as soon as she reached for him, he shut her down. His face would close up like it did, with his brow furrowing and his dark eyes flashing some unknown warning.

It left Hannah wondering what she had done wrong. Liam had been the one to want her, right? But now that had all come to a screeching halt. Maybe what Cole had mentioned was right. Maybe it was just a sex thing and now that there were other women available, Liam was no longer interested. Fair enough. So why did it leave Hannah feeling so twisted up?

With a frustrated huff, Hannah shoved the covers aside and sat up. Leaning forward she clutched her head in her hands and squeezed her eyes shut. Damn it, this was not natural. It was not the way it should be. She shouldn't love Cole so much and yet want Liam at the same time. She had to find some way to make it stop.

Crossing to the fireplace, Hannah stooped to place another small log on the hot coals. Then she grabbed a few candles and lit the wicks, bringing some dim lighting to the room. She didn't have a table in here, nor a desk, like Liam, but she had brought a few projects home just the same.

Rummaging around in the bottom dresser drawer, Hannah pulled out a pair of jeans and her sewing kit. It was the third pair she had cut down and re-stitched to fit a woman. When she was finished with them then Lena, Flynn and herself would each have two pairs of pants. Yes, she wasn't going to leave Flynn out just to spite her, though the thought had crossed her mind.

Smirking to herself, Hannah crawled back up on the bed and sat crosslegged. She brought the jeans onto her lap and took up where she had left off. Pushing the needle through the fabric, then out the other side, then through the fabric, then out the other side. Her stitches had been too loose and haphazard at first, but now she was well-practiced. The seams had to be strong or everything would just fall apart, so she took her time.

The work served to distract her at first, but eventually

her mind began to wander once more. They were running out of thread, not to mention spare clothes. Some of the guys were going to need fresh pants in a few months and now there weren't any to choose from.

When she had mentioned it to Cole, he had simply nodded and scratched at his cheek. His mind was elsewhere these days and he seemed to be going in a million different directions all at once. Nighttime was when he used to confide in her, let his thoughts unravel with his heavy leg thrown over her body in bed. But they didn't have that now, and she wondered how much longer he could keep this schedule up. He barely slept at all.

After what seemed a long time, her fingers were sore and her eyes itchy. She completed the last pair of pants and returned her work to its spot in the dresser. She should be tired now. Tired enough to banish the thoughts of Liam and fall asleep.

But her body... well it had other things planned, because her feet just kept pacing and her mind flailed around for excuses to show up at his cabin. She just needed to know. She had agreed to make herself available to him every two days and she needed to know if he still wanted that or not.

Maybe with Lena always around, Liam wasn't able to share whatever was on his mind. Now would be the perfect time to approach him. Although it was late... he was probably asleep, but hey, she was feeling desperate.

So before she had a chance to talk herself out of it,

Hannah snatched at her coat and slipped into her boots. She blew out both candles and checked the grate around the fire. It was safe enough, she judged. Steeling herself, she shoved out the front door and closed it with a decided snap behind her. The sharp noise echoed in the absolute quiet of the night.

Glancing up at the moon, Hannah wondered at the time and figured it had to be around midnight, maybe even later than that. *What are you doing?* Her mind was screaming at her but all the while her boots just kept on going like they had a mind of their own. They weren't afraid to take her where she wanted to go.

Aiming straight up the rocky incline and into the bunches of familiar trees Hannah arrived at Liam's cabin before she knew it. It was so very dark inside. No candles flickered, and why would they? It was late as hell.

Panting, Hannah made a lame attempt at collecting herself as she stared at the wooden door. Was she really about to knock on this thing? He was obviously asleep. Maybe she should come back?

But then her hand just flew out in front of her and there she was, rapping on the door. Holy crap, what am I doing? she thought, then nibbled at her lip. Inside, she heard a rustling sound, then heavy feet approaching.

When the door swung open, a sleep mussed Liam blinked down at her. Why was he so hot, with that square clean jaw and thick crop of dark hair? Hannah couldn't fight the instant smile that appeared on her face at the moment Liam registered her presence. His eyes popped wide, but then he was stepping outside and pulling the door closed behind him.

Hannah's mouth dropped a bit in shock, realizing that instead of drawing her in with him, he was shutting her out. Her heart tripped uncertainly and it took everything she had to attempt a lame recovery.

"Is everything alright?" Liam whispered, his face awash with concern.

"Um…" Hannah groped blindly for a reason to be here, but could find none. "I'm sorry. This was a mistake."

Whirling on her heel, she began a messy retreat. Her steps landed heavily, sending branches to snap and rocks to tumble. All she could hear was her own heart thumping loudly in her ears. How could she be so stupid?

Stupid. Stupid. Embarrassed. Stupid. Tears burned at the back of her eyes but she bit down on the inside of her cheek to successfully hold them at bay.

"Wait, Hannah-" Liam was just behind her, grabbing her wrist and spinning her around to face him. "Is everything okay? Are you hurt? Did you have another flashback?"

"No." Hannah couldn't help but laugh and shake her head. The heat on her wrist from where his hand still grasped her was unmistakeable and she had to break the contact. "I'm fine, really."

"Then what's this all about?" Liam's eyes narrowed as she wrenched her hand away.

"She's in there right? Lena?" Hannah asked, and she saw the answer form in his eyes.

"Wait, Hannah-"

"No. No, really." Hannah put up her hands, backing away from him, down the hill. "I have no right to feel like this. Between Cole and you, obviously I'm a complete hypocrite. You know what? Just forget I even came up here, okay? Just forget it."

"Hannah, wait."

Then giving up all pride in general, Hannah turned quickly and ran. She skidded and skipped down the remaining slope until she landed hard on the flat ground of the clearing. There was no time to pause, no time to look back as she zeroed in on Cole's cabin and moved fast to lock herself inside.

The fire had taken off so it felt instantly hot. Beads of sweat danced along Hannah's brow and she swiped at them with the sleeve of her jacket. A moment later, she heard Liam's gentle knock.

Scrunching up her face, she felt the flood of embarrassment swamp her full force. Of course he would come to try to make it all better. *Ugh, why?*

"Hannah, please let me in," Liam's voice was quiet, with an underlying pleading quality that reverberated in her mind.

Then it wasn't Liam's voice she was hearing. And it wasn't Cole's cabin she was standing in. The memory came on strong, like they always did at first, like she was living them over again.

. . .

*"P*LEASE, H*ANNAH* M*AE, JUST LET ME IN. I KNOW YOU'RE PISSED,*
but come on."

She was standing in her apartment, the one she shared with
Flynn and Lena. No one else was home.

Looking around, the place was clean and neat, with a long
gray couch and glass coffee table. But it was the voice coming
from the other side of the front door that captured all of her
focus. And she was properly pissed at that voice. That familiar
voice that she loved to distraction.

"Mom made you promise never to leave me behind," Hannah
choked on the words, knowing it was a low blow to bring up their
dead mother, but still.

She had been here for all of four years, and it hadn't taken
long for Uriah to start talking escape. She'd helped her brother
plan, had offered suggestions, had even run distractions for him
so he could gather more intel. Now after all of that, and one little
microchip, he was going to abandon her. The idea struck a
mutual chord of terror and anger inside her body.

"I believe that was when you were nine and wanted to tag
along to the movies." Uriah leaned his stout frame against the
door. She could see it give just a little, hear the groan of the wood.

Being eight years younger, Hannah had been the little leech
her older brother just couldn't get rid of. She idolized him, and
his cool friends and the fact he could drive and had a phone.
Somehow her feeling of awe in regards to him had never
completely gone away.

Taking her silence for weakness, he made his move. As
always, his voice was a whisper, "I need you to stay here. I need
you to wait for me, okay? It's important. Your name won't get

paired while I'm gone. Please, Hannah Mae, if you let me in, then we could talk for real."

By "talk" he meant hand writing words on paper, in the blind spots, away from the cameras and the microphones. Hannah's body slumped, knowing this could be the last time she might see him.

No, she wasn't going to think like that. He was a soldier, he knew what he was doing. He would come back for her, just like he said. Squaring her shoulders, Hannah sucked in a breath and unlocked the door.

"Hannah, please let me in, I can explain," Liam said, and rolled his eyes, knowing how tired that sounded.

With a shiver, he wrapped one arm around his body and tried knocking again. It was cold as fuck and he hadn't had time to grab his jacket, let alone pants. So here he was, standing in unlaced boots, boxers and a t-shirt. It had to be thirty degrees outside but he wasn't about to let the cold deter him. At least not yet.

"Come on, I'm sleeping on the floor," Liam offered. *Although you actually have sex with my best friend, but whatever, you're still pissed and you're a chick and that's kind of what you guys do.*

Pressing his ear to the door, Liam heard a thump and it sent his heart skipping in his chest. Had she fallen? If she would just open the damn door, then he could think straight without freezing his balls off.

He knocked harder, then waited. She was crying now,

the sounds of her quiet sniffling made its way through the locked door. Since when did Cole have an actual lock on this thing? Damn it.

Jumping from one foot to the other, Liam rubbed at his bare arms and cursed under his breath. It was Cole's fault this whole situation had nose dived anyway. He's the one who insisted Liam babysit Lena, even suggesting Liam bring her to sleep at his place.

Which Liam *had* done and admittedly the goal of getting her to talk was inching steadily closer. The little raven-haired girl was revealing more tidbits all the time and Liam was this close to broaching the subject of the code printed on her back. Despite Chan's scowl of disapproval and Liam's original protests, it turned out Cole's strategy had been a good one... again.

Of course the jerk had been pretty scarce lately himself, taking on all night watch shifts and dancing between the team members like a damn marionette. Cole was doing the work of four at this point.

With Ace and Ryder out of rotation for obvious reasons and then Liam had to be with Lena all the time. Not to mention Davey was pretty distracted on top of it. Sure the guy cut wood and hauled water, but he was slow as shit about it, and half the time he didn't get the entire job done. It was the dead of winter, and here they were... scrambling.

So every time Hannah had come around, Liam had been preoccupied handling Lena. He hadn't gotten the chance to talk privately with Cole about their little sharing arrangement and when a good time would be to go public with it.

Of course Liam figured Flynn would have something bitchy to say about it but he had no clue how Lena would react. Scratch that… she would probably be afraid they'd make her do the same thing. Which they wouldn't. Of course they wouldn't.

"Come on Hannah, please." Liam leaned his forehead against the door, unable to stop the shaking in his body.

"I'm asking you to just leave me alone, okay?"

"Shit. Look, I'm going to be right back." Liam paused, listening for a response, but when he didn't get any he high-tailed it back to his cabin.

If he was going to play the begging game then he was damn sure going to do it with pants and a heavy jacket on. He hadn't gotten a lot of time to know Hannah yet, and he suspected it would take some talking to sway her. At this point he was just thankful to have the opportunity.

Over the past week, there had been times he'd wondered if he was ever going to get another chance with her at all. The reasons the three of them had for agreeing to share in the first place just weren't the same anymore. There were two more women here now and apparently tens of thousands of them behind a Godforsaken fortress of metal further north.

Of course it also contained Nor Side soldiers, but they had been that too once. Well, at least until they had defected. Fuck. This wasn't going to be easy no matter how they swung it.

Quickening his already long strides, Liam breached the door to the cabin and closed it decidedly behind him. The fire was practically out, but the temperature inside felt like a furnace compared to the last twenty minutes of exposure.

"Everything alright?" Lena's tiny voice broke through the dark.

"Yeah, just go back to sleep."

"What is it?" Lena sat up. He could barely see her silhouette in the waning light from the window.

"Nothing, I'm going to get dressed and go out for a bit. No need to worry."

Liam tried to reassure her, but felt his chest tighten when instead of lying down, she shoved at the blankets and moved to get off the bed. His sleeping bag was on the floor, just like he had told Hannah, and he slept there every night. Even given more time it'd stay that way.

It wasn't that Lena wasn't a pretty girl, because truthfully she was. With her face cleared of bruising and her skin flushing healthy with a steady diet of food, she was attractive, becoming more so as the days went on. But damn it, she reminded him of… well…

And there was just something about Hannah that got to him. She made him feel things other than anger and death. Like actually *feel*. He just couldn't leave it alone.

"Well, I'll go with you," Lena said.

"No." Liam fought the panic that wanted to edge into his tone. It was too late for this shit, way too late for juggling women. "I mean, it's cold out and late. I'll be back soon."

"I know this sounds crazy," Lena's voice cracked. "But I'd rather follow you around in a blizzard then wait here for someone to come get me. I know… I know…"

"There's no one here to hurt you." Liam tried to assure her, but he could already hear her breath increasing. She was panicking, of course she was panicking, she'd been through a lot. He should have thought of that. "Listen, calm down. Just breathe…"

"Don't leave me. Please, just let me follow. I won't get in the way. Don't leave me. Just don't leave."

It was when she started to hiccup, coughing and sputtering, that Liam finally crossed to her and laid a tentative hand on her shoulder. Lena buried her face in his chest, working to suck in oxygen and stay quiet all at the same time. She was practically hyperventilating at the thought of him leaving her alone and yet she felt she had to be silent about it.

Guilt rushed through Liam's bloodstream as he wrapped his arms around her trembling body and stroked her back. He couldn't leave her like this, and he damn sure couldn't bring her down to Cole's cabin.

Shifting to sit on the bed, Liam drew her onto his lap and let her cry. All the while he whispered to her, letting her know it was okay. It was okay to make noise. It was okay to be afraid. No one was ever going to hurt her again.

They were words Liam knew by heart. Words that came to him, like a voice speaking right beside his ear. Because they were his own mother's words. And at the time she had spoken them to Liam, she hadn't known they were lies. She didn't know that night would be the last of her life, but Liam would never forget it.

THE NEXT DAY DAWNED BRIGHT AND EARLY. LIAM WAS BACK on the floor with a splitting headache working right behind his eyes. If only there was such a thing as a day off around here. But there wasn't. Not when other people's survival depended on you getting the job done. And there were always jobs that needed doing.

Whether it be wood, water, or watch duty. Liam let a rueful smile light his lips. Throw in a tour of the pasture, perimeter fence, hay for the livestock, food prep, clean up, the list went on. Not to mention Liam hadn't been able to work in his shop in forever. Not since they'd left on the rescue.

The palm of his hand was just itching to roll a knife against it. He had plans in his head for a dozen new designs now and he figured if he fancied up the hilts, he could probably trade for even more goods in the city. Cole had mentioned the need for a supply run. They had more mouths to feed and clothe than ever before. Plus, there were those rumors about a medicine stockpile. It wouldn't hurt to ask around.

"You up?" Lena's voice sounded out from the bed.

"Yeah," Liam answered, then rolled over with a groan and crawled out of his sleeping bag.

"Look, about last night-"

"You don't have to say anything." Liam yawned, covering his mouth half heartedly before crossing to his shelves and poking through his clothes.

"I feel like I do, though. I sort of broke down on you, and I'm sorry."

"It's fine." Liam grabbed a semi-dirty pair of pants and a set of fresh boxers. Laundry would have to go on the to do list as well, he thought. "Don't look, I'm changing."

"Oh," Lena exclaimed, and he heard her shift around on the mattress. "Well, anyway I just thought I owed you an explanation."

"You don't." Liam zipped up his pants and pulled his shirt over his head before tossing it to the floor. "I'm decent, you can look."

"Okay." Again he heard Lena shifting.

When he rotated to face her, Liam grimaced at her beaten expression. Why was his default mode always set to asshole? Sucking in a breath, he ran a hand down his face.

"I'm the one who should be sorry," Liam admitted finally. "You've got something to say, then please say it. I'll listen."

Blinking at him from her position on the bed, Lena's black hair was tangled from sleep but her large blue eyes were crystal clear. She tugged absently at the oversized cotton shirt Liam had loaned her, then folded her legs even further beneath her body before ducking her head.

"I've been afraid every single day since I walked away from the Wall." Lena swallowed, her fingers tracing nervous circles on the twisted blankets. "I can't tell you how many times I wished for it all to be over. For every-thing to just end, you know?"

Lifting her head, she locked eyes with Liam for a moment, and he couldn't help but nod. Yeah, he knew what that felt like, that sort of fear.

"Even when you all came, I thought it would be just like before," Lena admitted, her eyes a pool of shame. "I wished for Ryder to die while he was bleeding in the snow. I hoped he would die, that you all would die."

"Lena, that's-"

"No." Lena held up her hands, cutting him off. "Please let me finish. It wasn't until you took *him* to the shed and started… you know. That was the first glimmer of hope I had felt in so long. Listening to him crying, that was some-thing I didn't know how badly I needed."

"How you felt-" Liam breached the silence. "About Ryder dying, that was completely normal. You don't have to feel ashamed about it."

"Thank you." Lena nodded, her lips trembled a moment, then firmed. "The moment we stepped foot inside this compound, and you were assigned to watch me, that's the first time I felt less fear. It's not gone completely, I don't know if it ever will be, but it's tolerable.

Whenever I'm with you, I can breathe. I know it sounds ridiculous but you make the fear stop hurting so bad. That's why I freaked out when you wanted to leave last night. It's because the fear just came rushing back, and I felt like I was going to drown in it. I'm sorry."

Well, shit. Liam scratched at his five o-clock shadow and let loose a sigh.

Shifting his eyes to the ceiling, he wondered at the spot he found himself in. He was a simple man, truly, at least that's how he liked to see himself. Since the war, the only things that had mattered to him were Cole's family and the job. Then there was just Cole, the team, and the job. And it had gone on like that for *years*.

He was a ruthless killer. He was a monster who strung men up by the ankle after he'd gutted them. He was a grade A level 1 asshole. Right?

"Then I won't leave you," Liam said, eyes dropping back down to rest on Lena. "At least not until you're ready."

THE FIRST RAYS OF A NEW DAY'S SUN WERE JUST MAKING their presence known. Tipping his face towards the east, Cole watched the progress through tired eyes. It had been another quiet night, and cold. It was always cold.

Wedging his hands further into the pockets of the watch coat, Cole huffed a breath and stood up to stretch. The one wooden chair on the platform wasn't supposed to be comfortable. The idea of a watch shift was to stay awake, but still… now his whole body ached instead of just his eyes.

A low whistle sounded below him, but it didn't take Cole by surprise. After all, what good would he be up here if he didn't notice the things that went on below him?

Stepping to the rope ladder, Cole shoved it through the hole in the platform using the side of his boot and then glanced down. Trey was jumping a bit on the ground, trying to warm up his body against the chill of an early morning. They would need about another week of this schedule Cole judged, before he could safely transition them back to how it was before.

Ryder had finally stabilized. He was sitting up for short periods and eating food like there was no tomorrow. When Cole had last checked, he could see the relief that filled both Ace and Flynn's faces. They hadn't been sure he would pull through. In fact, they had almost counted the kid out.

A grim line worked itself across Cole's mouth. The truth was, the team had been that close to losing Ryder, and as usual it would have been all Cole's fault. He should never have left the kid with Hannah. He should've known it would be too much for him to be left behind.

With a shake of his head, Cole dismissed the guilt. Trey was nearing the top.

"Right on time," Cole commented, reaching through the manhole to grab Trey's rifle.

"Yeah," Trey exhaled and hoisted his body the rest of the way through. "Old habits die hard."

"Still not sleeping well?"

"Nah." Trey shook his head and rolled his shoulders.

Seemed like each of them had their own separate issue. Cookie yammered and made meals to avoid the faces. Liam stalked around like a panther. Trey couldn't sleep. Chan didn't talk. The list of repercussions went on and on. But it was like that with war, wasn't it?

"So, I'll send Chan up after lunch." Cole shrugged out of

the watch coat and slung his own rifle across his back. "You need anything to eat?"

"Nah." Trey grunted again before patting his pockets, they bulged with jerky and hard tac.

"Suit yourself." Cole sighed before crouching down to lower himself through the hole in the platform. Just as he hooked his feet in the rungs, Trey spoke.

"Is it true?" He asked, causing Cole to look up. "Hannah can't remember anything?"

"Yeah," Cole squinted up at the other man. "It's true."

"And Flynn," Trey continued. "She's not talking. Not saying anything else about the refugee center? The Wall?"

"Not yet," Cole admitted. "But we'll find out soon, Trey. And I'll make sure everyone knows the truth. Okay?"

"Yeah," Trey bobbed his head. "Thanks, boss."

As he descended, Cole's hands absorbed the icy chill of the rope ladder. It was a fairly long way down, maybe about thirty feet. The shifting rungs that sagged with each step didn't make it any easier, but Cole didn't hardly notice. He had climbed up and down its length more times than he could recall. Besides, Trey's questions were now filling his mind.

The team was talking, trading stories and theories. This sort of murmuring wouldn't go away, quite the opposite, in fact. Given time, the talk would build and become dangerous in its own right. Cole needed to provide them with honest answers; answers that he himself did not yet have.

By the time his boots touched ground, Cole's mind was clicking a million miles an hour. A few days ago, Hannah had another flashback. It was the night she and Liam had argued. Cole had been on watch and heard them, though he swore to himself he wouldn't interfere. It was one of Hannah's little rules so he had turned away, done his best to ignore them.

But when Cole arrived home that morning, the front door had been locked. When he pressed Hannah about it, she had been reluctant to provide him with any details. Except in the end she did admit to having another memory. He wondered now if she would've told him about the flashback at all, if she hadn't forgotten to unlock the door.

Even so, what she did tell him was vague. She remembered living behind the Wall, but only briefly. She'd been arguing with her brother. His name was Uriah. Something about him leaving and not taking her with him.

Supposedly that was it but Cole had known Hannah long enough now, he could tell she was holding back. The realization in turns frustrated and unnerved him.

Cole had been meaning to talk to Liam about it but the chance hadn't yet presented itself. If anyone could get more information out of Hannah, it was him. And on that front, the living situation with Flynn and Lena would need to be formally addressed.

Now that they were finally out of crisis mode with Ryder, Cole felt he could apply more pressure to the little redheaded nurse. That would be the priority for today, he decided, *after* he caught a couple hours sleep.

Never one to miss an opportunity though, Cole took the long way around back to his cabin. He paced the perimeter fence, dodging bushes and the last tiny remnants of snow that collected beneath the towering pines. When he reached the front gate, he paused, checking for tracks on the far side.

Nothing fresh, he noted, before doubling back and heading for the clearing. Most everything was quiet. Aside from himself, Trey and Cookie, the compound was still sleeping.

All the cabins were dark, with no smoke drifting from their makeshift chimneys. Only Cookie could be heard, banging around in the storage building. They had transferred the dishes and cooking utensils up to the stone house finally. Not the bulk of the food, though, it had to stay down in the cellar.

With the older man awake, that meant breakfast wouldn't be too far off. Cole wasn't sure if he'd make it that long, though. Despite his stomach's grumbling, his eyes were heavy and his shoulders slumped just a touch. When he got to his front door, Cole exhaled a breath when it shoved open easily. No lock this time.

Hannah stirred on the bed, but didn't wake. As quietly as possible, he shut the door behind him and added a few more logs to the fire. He would need to haul more wood inside soon, but he could do that later.

Stepping out of his boots, Cole shed his clothes and lifted the edge of the blankets on the mattress. Hannah was beautiful in her sleep. Hair tangled messily, her night shirt pulled up slightly to reveal the soft skin of her thighs.

Carefully, he slid down next to her and laid his head on the pillow beside hers. She murmured briefly as he pulled her warm body up against his cold one. Burying his face in the back of her neck, he exhaled. Within seconds, he was out.

A FEW HOURS LATER, COLE ROLLED OVER WITH A GROAN. Stretching one arm across the bed, he found the mattress cool and empty. Hannah was gone.

Picking up his head, Cole glanced briefly around the small room. The fire was burning pleasantly but he was decidedly alone. With a sigh he flopped onto his back and brought both of his hands to his forehead. The sun was shining through the trees outside his window. The wind gusted, rattling the glass pane slightly. First order of business, he thought, track down Liam.

Shoving the covers back, Cole swung his legs to the floor and crossed to his dresser. He rifled through his meager collection of clothes and selected a clean shirt and pants. Now that Hannah lived with him, he no longer had to worry about doing laundry, although she had taken nearly half of his shirts as her own. Underwear and socks, too.

Their supply was running painfully thin. All the more

reason to make another supply run. Cole grimaced. He would have preferred not to do it in the dead of winter.

Running a hand over his face, Cole itched at his beard absently and eyed the pair of scissors laying on top of the dresser. He could use a trim, and not just of his beard, either. His hair was falling down into his eyes now. But it would have to wait. There just wasn't enough time in the day as it was.

Lacing up his boots, Cole glanced over at the fire. The flames rumbled safely behind the grate so he could leave it. After donning his jacket, he shoved outside and into the bright sunlight.

Overhead, a collection of clouds dotted in the distance. With the breeze going like it was, it wouldn't be long before they were under their gray cover. But this brief glimpse of sun was a nice change, even if it wouldn't last all day.

Eyes absorbing the compound quickly, Cole sucked air into his lungs. It still had that icy chill in it. To his left, Davey was standing at the entrance to the storage shed, his foot wedged strategically to keep the door open.

His focus was on what lay inside, or rather, who. There was someone just beyond the door, Cole could hear the other person rummaging around.

"Well, what do we have?" Davey asked, his arms already overflowing with folded blankets.

"Nothing that would work," Chan called out.

"It doesn't have to be big," Davey again.

"What doesn't?" Cole interjected, closing the short distance between them.

"Oh hey." Davey huffed a breath as he nodded at Cole. "We didn't want to wake you."

"Morning, Chan," Cole called, leaning his head into the darkened space.

The other man merely scowled before giving up a curt nod. Things hadn't been right between the two of them for a while now. Cole had been meaning to take Chan aside and get to the bottom of it but like so many other things, it had been tabled in favor of bigger issues.

"So, what are you guys looking for?" Cole cleared his throat, eyes shifting back to Davey.

"We're making another tub for the stone house," Davey explained. "For the girls to wash in and also for laundry."

"Oh." Cole straightened. "That's a good idea."

"Yeah, but we were thinking a washboard of some kind would make it easier," Davey elaborated, shifting the bundle in his arms. "And maybe a drain plug with a pipe or a hose."

Cole grunted and stepped back, eyes popping up to the roof line of the storage shed. It was made of tin. They had taken the sheets from the farmhouse. The metal was corrugated and though it had rusted a bit over the years, the underside was still relatively clean. It had the ripples one would want for a washboard.

"We could cut a small square from the back," Cole suggested, pointing up as Davey followed his line of sight.

"I think the rear corner has an overlapping section that would be just big enough."

"That'd work." Davey nodded, still eyeing the metal. "I could frame it with wood, maybe even make two."

Chan came out to stand between them. He had his hands fisted on his hips as he tilted his face up to access the roof line. Cole couldn't help but note the neat cut to his hair and freshly shaven face. The tension he carried though, that lingered through his shoulders and the clench of his jaw.

"I'll get the shears and a ladder," Chan announced.

"Need help?" Cole asked, though he knew the answer before the question leapt from his mouth.

"No."

They stood there in silence for a few moments, the three of them staring up at the roof. Cole worked to keep his face easy and the string of words he wanted to say held tightly inside his mouth. Whatever was going on, he just couldn't deal with it right this very moment. Chan was pissed. Had been pissed. Would remain pissed for a while longer.

After a beat, Cole turned on a swivel and walked away. Sometimes the best thing you can do with family is ignore them. And that's how Cole felt about each one of his guys. They were his family now, his only family. No matter what.

As Cole climbed up the hill, his arms swinging at his sides, he glanced occasionally at Liam's cabin. No smoke puffed above it but that wasn't so unusual for this time of day now.

There had been a time when Liam could perpetually be found hammering away in his shed. The ting of iron striking metal had echoed with consistency all over the compound. But now the small building stood silent, as it had for too long.

Cole frowned at the realization as he stepped up to the front door of Liam's cabin and pulled it open. He only wanted to confirm what he already knew, Liam wasn't home. Just as he suspected, the space was hollow and dark.

Stepping back, Cole was just about to shut the door when a glint of silver caught his eye. There was something small on the tabletop. Cole frowned, he didn't know Liam had a desk, nor a bed frame for that matter. Quickly, Cole took the few steps necessary to enter the space and plucked up the shining bracelet.

It was small, and pretty. The etching was clearly done by hand. Cole recognized the work immediately as something Liam had made. Nice, he thought, before replacing it. They could trade a lot of goods for it maybe, in the city.

Back outside, Cole headed further up the hill, his boots aiming for the stone house. Smoke rose clearly through the thick of trees just above it. Maybe Cookie had saved him a bite of food, he thought.

Stomach rumbling, Cole heard the far off chop of an axe. As he walked, he listened to the steady rhythm of a blade striking wood, over and over. At least someone was working hard today.

When he reached the stone house, Cole stopped short. An expansive smile plastered itself unwittingly across his face. Someone had moved two chairs out in the sun and there was his Hannah, holding tight onto Ryder's hand. The pair of them sat side by side, Ryder wrapped in a big blanket, his eyes closed against the brightness of the light.

"Guess they let him walk a few steps today, huh?" Cole asked as he approached them.

"They didn't *let* me do anything," Ryder responded, his voice was gravely, but strong. "I told them they couldn't keep me tied down in there a second longer."

"You're giving the orders, then." Cole bobbed his head, working to clear his throat, it was suddenly too tight. "That's good, buddy. That's real good."

Through everything that had happened, the raid and subsequent stabbing, the trek home and weeks of waiting, Cole hadn't ever felt like this. The swelling that now gripped his chest, the burning in his throat, the feelings were so old, he didn't hardly recognize them for what they were. Relief. That and the overwhelming urge to cry.

With a shake of his head, Cole let his eyes drop to where Hannah patted calmly at the back of Ryder's hand. The kid was alive, sitting in the peaceful sunlight with a woman holding his hand. This is the thing they had all wanted, right? This was the task they had set out to accomplish.

Cole shoved back at the flood of his emotions. Weakness. That was all it was. He suppressed the hope and happiness, the stab of guilt and sorrow until they were all just a comfortable ugly ball in the pit of his stomach once more. When he finally looked up, he was perfectly composed.

"Have you seen Liam?" He asked, and watched Hannah's pleasant expression fall briefly into a frown as she looked away. So, they were still on the outs after their fight. Well, Cole would stay out of it, just like he had sworn to do.

"He's making a bathtub," Ryder answered. His pale-blue eyes looked tired, he couldn't hardly keep them open.

"How long have you been out here?" Cole asked.

"Not long enough," Ryder quipped, but then couldn't help the way his jaw dropped, letting out a little panting breath.

"I'm getting pretty tired myself," Hannah interjected.

She turned her face towards Ryder, leaning in and whispering to him. Cole watched her golden hair fall back as her hand came up to feel Ryder's forehead. The kid tried to pull away, but only for a split second. Eyes fluttering, he quickly gave up under Hannah's soft touch.

Ryder had so much fight in him, Cole realized. He had fought like hell to stay alive but the battle wasn't nearly over. No, it was only that he was finally winning now, that's all. And they had to help him win.

"Ace inside?" Cole asked.

"Yes." Hannah glanced at Cole with a worried expression. "Go get him?"

"On it."

Cole left them and shoved his way into the stone house. It was substantially warmer than outside, with the fire roaring and the smell of lunch cooking in the air. Flynn was sitting at the table, her hands working a needle and thread through a pale-green checked shirt. She looked up at his arrival.

"Time's up?" She asked, seeming to know what Cole was there for by instinct alone.

"Yeah."

IN THE END IT TOOK THREE OF THEM TO HAUL RYDER BACK to his bunk. Ace, Cookie and Cole all worked together to hoist the chair up with the kid still sitting in it. Ryder had protested at first, issuing a steady string of curses as he failed in an attempt to stand and walk inside by himself.

But then Flynn and Hannah had fluttered about, coaxing and cajoling until the kid was so overwhelmed with feminine nagging that he gave in and used the last of his strength to brace himself in his seat. Once they laid him back down on his belly in the bunk he managed a few bites of soup before dropping into sleep.

While he was out, Flynn lifted his shirt so both she and Ace could check over his wounds. The rest of them stepped back to watch.

Five ugly pink slashes of skin, all puckered with stitches, were healing nicely. Flynn had been the one to stitch him up, looping the needle and thread expertly through his flesh weeks ago.

Cole could still hear the quality of Ryder's screaming

that night, at least until he had passed out. But his wounds were cleaned up now and though obviously still painful, they were looking good. At least the nurse and the medic were both nodding.

Once satisfied, Ace stood up and offered a hand to Flynn who took it. Back on her feet, the little redhead dusted off her palms and glanced over her shoulder.

Hannah stiffened under the other woman's gaze but she did not look away. Cole reached for her hand.

"I could tell you all about yourself, you know," Flynn commented, turning around to face them, arms folded across her chest. "I could answer all of your questions. I lived with you for years."

Hannah didn't respond. The room filled with a tense sort of silence. Ace and Cookie said nothing, though their eyes skipped between the two women, waiting. Cole readied himself to intervene.

"But you don't like me," Hannah countered finally. "How do I know you're telling the truth?"

"It wasn't always that way," Flynn supplied. "And Lena could be there, too. She could vouch for what I said."

"Why would you do that?" Hannah was cautious. Cole held his breath.

"I want answers, too." Flynn waited a beat, eyes darting from Hannah to Cole and back. "But we'd have to be alone when we talked. Who knows, maybe it will even help you remember more."

The little redhead's eyes sparkled with some knowing

quality. Cole frowned. He wouldn't let her hurt his Hannah. He wouldn't give her the chance.

Just then, Hannah loosened her grip on his hand. She was just about ready to step forward. She was just about ready to agree to Flynn's terms when Cole yanked her back.

"No deal," he said, and felt the grumbling disagreement from Ace before the other man even opened his mouth.

CHAPTER FIFTEEN_
HANNAH

IT WAS DARK OUT, DINNER WAS SIMMERING, AND THEY STILL hadn't stopped arguing. From the moment Flynn made her offer, Hannah knew it would go down this way. She knew Cole would refuse and she knew the team would rally against him. They wanted answers. *Everyone* here wanted answers, in one form or another.

And at the moment they weren't getting any. Lena wouldn't talk without Flynn's consent. Flynn wouldn't talk unless she was alone with Hannah. Hannah wouldn't talk without Cole's consent. Cole wouldn't give it.

And so the war raged. It was hard to listen to. It was hard to let Cole go on this way, but she did. The truth was, she needed this extra time in order to strategize. Because Hannah's recent memory of her brother had changed things for her. That last conversation they'd had before Uriah left the Wall, it sparked something for her. Something bigger than she yet understood.

So in the end, no matter what Cole agreed to or didn't, the cold fact remained… Hannah needed to talk to Flynn… and it *had* to be alone. But publicly she couldn't go against Cole, so they were officially stuck.

Sitting at the long wooden table, Hannah kept her hands folded demurely in her lap. Everyone had been called in for this display, everyone. It was an emergency team meeting of sorts, no one was even on watch.

Liam and Lena had come down from cutting wood, looking all dusty and sweaty despite the cold weather. It was the dark-haired woman who sat across from Hannah now, but she faced away from her, watching Liam, like always.

Trey leaned against the far wall, eyes tracking the situation while Cookie bent over the fireplace and heated up day old stew.

"But what's the harm in letting them talk?" Ace persisted. His dark skin was flushed and his cheeks heated with resolve.

"Alone?" Cole was incredulous. "Do I really need to spell it out? It's not safe. *We* still don't get any answers. It puts Hannah in danger."

"From what I've heard, Hannah can handle herself," Ace countered. "So we watch through a window."

"No." Cole shook his head for the millionth time. "I'm in the same room, or nothing at all."

Chan shifted in his seat. He was right beside Hannah, his expression impassive though his eyes were intent. He watched the exchange with interest before letting his eyes drift for a moment to linger on Lena's back.

The other woman stirred but did not turn around. If she could feel his eyes on her, she gave no indication.

"What do you think, Chan?" Hannah whispered, causing him to jump slightly. It was like he had forgotten she sat there beside him.

"I want to know what's behind the Wall." Chan let his brown eyes cross to hers. "Don't you?"

The question was an interesting one and it flooded Hannah's brain for several moments. Yes, of course she wanted the full story… because despite her flashbacks, she still didn't have it.

But Hannah knew just enough now to make her extra cautious. There were bigger things going on. Things that maybe Cole and the others shouldn't know about. And after all, it was Uriah she had to protect at all costs. That's what she had remembered.

"Dinner's ready," Cookie called. "Let's take a break and eat. Something tells me we're gonna be at this all night."

There were grumbles all around. Some in agreement, some not. When Hannah made to stand, Cole caught her eye and motioned for her to sit back down. He would bring her a bowl.

Giving him a nod, she watched him turn his back and move to grab two dishes from the nearby shelf. The others shuffled over as well, submitting to Cookie's suggestion, maneuvering around one another, eyeing Cole.

"Well?" Chan's voice was low, his eyes appraising. He

hadn't moved from his seat. She hadn't answered his question.

"Yes." Hannah blinked at him. "Of course I want to know."

For several seconds they eyed one another. Chan keeping his face carefully blank while Hannah worked to keep her breathing even. She didn't like being under such scrutiny all of a sudden, and especially not from Chan. It was impossible to know what was going through his mind. It put her at a distinct disadvantage.

"You know what I think?" Chan asked, leaning forward.

"What?"

"I think you could put a stop to this whole thing right now if you wanted."

"Chan-"

"But you aren't," Chan cut her off, eyes flashing hot as his fingers continued to drum casually on the table. "I just haven't figured out why, yet."

Hannah's mouth hung open as Chan's face drifted from confrontational back into its normally blank state. It wasn't until Liam approached them that he finally shoved up to standing and walked away. Snapping her mouth closed, Hannah swallowed deliberately, watching the empty chair he had left for another beat.

"Everything alright?" Liam asked, pulling out a chair to sit beside Lena. The little dark-haired woman relaxed instantly as he settled down by her side and accepted the bowl of food he offered her.

"Of course." Hannah ducked her head, avoiding his searching eyes.

Liam's spoon hovered over his untouched bowl, his other hand splayed flat against the wooden surface of the table. She hadn't been this close to him since the night she had come to his cabin, a night she regretted entirely. Up to this point she had been successful in avoiding him and thereby saving herself from re-living her stupidity. Of course now here he was, staring.

Glancing up Hannah felt her cheeks flush and she was forced to look away once more.

"Hey." Cole set down two bowls and pulled out the chair next to her.

"Hey," Hannah answered, feeling a mix of guilt and appreciation for him.

Here he was, protecting her as usual, and she wasn't even willing to give him the whole story. It was just that, Hannah didn't know enough yet herself. She didn't want to make a mistake. She didn't want to put her brother at risk by saying the wrong thing to the wrong people. Reaching out her hand, she spread her palm across his thigh as he took a seat and inched his chair closer.

"Eat," Cole commanded.

As he slid her bowl squarely in front of her, Hannah couldn't help but give him a smile. He was a good man, really he was. And she trusted him with her own life, so why couldn't she trust him with her brother's?

Because he's a Nor Side Soldier. You don't know where his

true loyalty lies. The voice from inside was a strong one, making her smile fade.

Dipping her spoon into the bowl, Hannah blew over the hot stew for a few seconds before tentatively bringing it to her lips. The food was hearty and thick with diced carrots, corn kernels and meat. She hadn't realized how hungry she was until now.

Steadily the table filled all around them. Flynn was at the far end, wedged between Ace and Davey. Every so often, Hannah could feel the other woman's eyes resting on her. But she didn't dare look over, not when the only sounds in the room were the scraping of spoons and the slurping of stew. Even Cookie and Trey remained silent, which was no small feat.

"I say we take a vote," Davey suggested, as the eating slowed.

"I don't see the point," Cole's voice was low but cutting. "This isn't a group decision."

"Like hell it's not." Ace leaned forward. "We need answers, all of us. This isn't just about you and Hannah."

"It's not happening."

"Just let us vote!" Voices were raised and others jumped in.

Trey, Davey, Ace, Cookie, Cole. They were all talking over each other until the words they said blurred and became indecipherable. Cole gripped Hannah's wrist under the table and held on tight. Ace stood up, bracing his hands on either side of his empty bowl.

Hannah's heart was pounding and she squeezed her

eyes shut, fighting the urge to get up and run out. She wanted answers, too, really she did, but she wouldn't go against Cole. If he wouldn't let her talk to Flynn alone, then no manner of voting would convince her to do so.

"Let me talk to them," Liam said, and had everyone stopping mid-sentence.

It was the first time he had spoken on the subject, which wasn't rare necessarily. When they had fetched him back to the stone house, Liam had come, but quietly so. Though Hannah had done her best to ignore him, she couldn't help noticing the way he whispered with Cole before taking up a position by the far door. And he hadn't moved from that spot, not until dinner had been announced.

Hannah felt the heat of his stare on her skin, so she opened her eyes and lifted her head. Sure enough, Liam was watching. His face was clean shaven, and for a split second, Hannah could almost feel the smoothness running beneath the tips of her fingers. Biting her lip in shame, she fidgeted uncomfortably and refocused on her bowl.

"What are you trying to say?" Ace prompted.

"Let me talk to each of them alone," Liam answered. But his words, like always, were too few. "I'll start with the nurse."

"Like talk to them or *talk* to them?" Ace's brow furrowed and the others shifted uncomfortably. Liam was an interrogator by trade, they all wondered at his methods here.

"It's fine," Lena offered. Turning to Liam, she rested a hand on his forearm. "He wouldn't hurt them."

Flynn huffed a laugh at that, crossing her arms over her chest. But the gesture, though defensive, didn't match up with her tone, which was accepting. The nurse trusted what Lena said, implicitly. After all, they had lived in hell together. Literal hell. That bond trumped any doubt.

"I'll go on one condition," Flynn announced, tipping back in her chair. "You're not allowed to ask me any questions using your knife."

The table rippled appreciatively at her humor and even Liam cracked a smile. Standing up, he dug around in his pocket and laid his large knife down on the table.

"Where to?" Flynn asked as she stood.

"The bunk room." Liam gestured to the darkened threshold.

"Ryder's in there."

"He's sleeping."

"No I'm not!" Ryder called, and had half the men groaning aloud. There went all opportunity for eavesdropping.

Flynn merely smirked at her triumph while Liam rolled his eyes.

"Guess we'll have to move him then," Liam countered.

But the frown on Ace's face stopped that thought dead in its tracks. Ryder had already pushed the envelope once today, sitting outside for an hour with Hannah monitoring his every breath. He had done okay in the end, but even that little outing had been heavily debated. The medic and nurse eyed one another briefly before Ace shook his head. They didn't want to risk moving him again.

"My place then," Liam offered, and had Flynn nodding in acceptance.

As they walked towards the front door together, Lena rose quickly and began to follow. Hannah watched the fluttering nervousness in the other woman's hands. The way she went to clutch at her own throat, but stopped short. When Liam looked behind him and spied her, his eyes darted to Flynn who gave him another nod. She would talk with Lena there, not a problem.

Hannah's stomach dipped and her mind raced. She wondered what Liam's reaction would be when she refused to let his newest companion come along. No, it didn't make any sense. No, it wasn't fair. But Hannah didn't want to see any more of Liam with Lena then she already did.

She didn't have long to dwell on the subject; however, before Cole was drawing her up and away from the table. He pulled her into the corner by the fireplace and ran a hand through her hair.

"You okay with this?" He asked. "You don't have to talk to Liam if you don't want to."

"I'll talk to him," Hannah assured him, reaching up to cup his hand in her own. If it was only Liam, then she felt she could manage well enough. She wouldn't tell him anything she didn't want to.

The time ticked by slowly it seemed, with everyone huddled together in their little groups. When Liam and the two women finally walked back in, Hannah was on edge. She hadn't yet decided what, if anything, she would tell him. This was his idea after all, not hers, and she wasn't sure how he planned on resolving the whole complicated situation.

As Flynn swept past, she didn't make eye contact, but wasn't overly huffy either. Glancing over her shoulder, Hannah watched the nurse walk back to the table and take a seat beside Ace. He placed a hand on her shoulder, and leaned in to say something. They had gotten close over the past weeks, caring for Ryder.

Liam stopped beside them then, with his little Lena lingering a few feet behind. Hannah let her eyes fall on the dark-haired woman. She was like a pretty china doll, all porcelain skin and vivid blue eyes.

"You want me to go?" Cole asked, and had Hannah's blood pumping. She knew he wouldn't like her answer so she dropped her eyes. Before she could shake her head though, Liam saved her.

"No, I need to talk to her one on one," Liam explained.

"You let Lena go with Flynn," Cole pointed out.

"That was different."

"How?"

"She knows everything Flynn has to say already," Liam provided.

"Oh, and you don't think I do?"

"Cole." Liam said his friend's name with that tone he

used. The one that always had Cole dialing back, re-thinking. Hannah chanced to look up and saw the men talking silently with only their eyes. They did this often, maybe more often than either of them realized.

"Fine." Cole threw up his hands and turned away.

At the same time, Liam's hand snaked out and clasped Hannah's. Her breath caught in her throat and before she could even blink he was turning around and tugging her out the door.

It was late in the night now and the darkness outside was heavy with mist. Though it was difficult to see, it didn't stop Liam. He didn't slow his steps or look back. He didn't let go of her either.

Obscure light from a half hidden moon lit the ground as Hannah tripped and stumbled in an attempt to keep up with him. His strides were long and sure as he headed down the slope to his cabin. By the time they breached his door and he released her inside, the heat from his contact had burned itself up her arm. Subconsciously, she clutched at her wrist, rubbing the spot where she could still feel his fingers wrapping her skin.

For Liam's part, he never stopped moving. He pulled the chair from beneath his desk and planted it firmly outside his front door. Hannah stood stunned, watching in wonder. What was going on?

A few short strands of Liam's dark hair fell forward over his forehead as he darted back inside and gathered several blankets off the bed. It wasn't until he turned back to the doorway that Hannah noticed Lena lingering outside. The other woman's face was creased with worry, but her eyes didn't leave Liam, not even for a second.

With his back to Hannah, Liam wrapped the blankets around Lena and gestured to the chair. The other woman gripped his forearm impulsively a moment before Liam leaned down to whisper quietly to her. After a brief exchange, Hannah watched the little fingers reluctantly release as the blanketed figure took a seat. Liam backed a few steps into the cabin, then slowly swung shut the wooden door.

"I can't talk with her here," Hannah spoke to Liam's back, watching his shoulders tense at her words.

"She's outside," Liam countered, turning to face her.

"She can still hear," Hannah reasoned, but only managed to hold Liam's gaze for a second.

"So we'll talk in the far corner." Liam took a step forward. "You can whisper."

"Liam-"

"She's scared, Hannah. Don't you remember what it's like to be scared?"

Raising her head, Hannah watched Liam shrug out of his jacket and toss it on the desk. It was warm in his cabin. The fire had been going for awhile and beads of sweat wanted to work their way down Hannah's back.

Anywhere else, with anyone else, Hannah would have taken her coat off. Not here though. Not now. Not with that heat still working up her arm and her heart jumping for him. She needed all the layers she could get around this man.

"You've been avoiding me." Liam tilted his head to one side as he edged closer to her.

"No." Hannah swallowed the lie.

A lopsided smile crossed Liam's face as he huffed a breath out through his nose. Giving his head a slight shake, he gestured to the remaining chair in the far corner. Hannah glanced over her shoulder at it.

"I'd rather stand," she said.

Straightening her shoulders, Hannah resolved to take control of the situation but when she turned back to Liam he was practically on top of her.

Forced to look up into his face, she sucked in a quick breath and backed a step. Those dark eyes of his bored into her and through her, the way they always did. How did he manage it? How could he make her whole body tense with just a look?

"What happened the other night?" Liam asked, his voice lowering until she had to strain to hear it.

"I don't know," Hannah breathed the words. "I wish I could take it back."

"Just that night... or everything with me?"

"Everything," Hannah answered, thinking maybe then she wouldn't feel this way.

If she had never slept with Liam, then maybe her heart wouldn't race every time he passed by. Maybe she wouldn't drown in her guilt every night she woke thinking of him. And she could finally be at peace, just loving Cole. Liam could be with his little Lena and Hannah wouldn't feel such a twisted mix of hate and shame.

Liam eyed her for a moment, his hand coming up to hover just beside her face. Unable to hold his gaze, Hannah closed her eyes as sweat poured down her back, her heart thumping painfully the whole while. Just when she expected to feel his fingers come down to stroke against her cheek, she heard him step back.

Exhaling, Hannah's eyes flew open in time to see Liam take a heavy seat on the edge of the bed. His face was composed, carefully so.

"Are you willing to talk to Flynn?" He asked.

"I want to speak to Flynn, but I want to do it alone."

"Seriously?" Liam looked at the ceiling a moment. "So it's only Cole holding you back?"

Hannah shrugged.

"And you'd never go against Cole," Liam supplied. "At least not publicly."

"Never."

"What changed for you?"

"What do you mean?"

"You weren't willing to talk to her before, something changed."

Hannah blinked at him a moment, her mind whirling through an array of acceptable answers, none of which would be the truth. Before she could settle on one, Liam had already come to his own conclusion.

"You've remembered something." Liam nodded knowingly. "Something both of you want to hide from us."

"No-"

"Stop, Hannah." Liam shoved up from the bed and

stalked over to her. "You may regret letting me inside you, but I wouldn't take back a single second of it. Nothing's changed for me. Do you really think that I wouldn't protect you?"

"But-"

"I'd protect you from all of them, including Cole," Liam kept his voice low, his face bent in close. Hannah could feel the whisper of his breath across her face.

"I had a flashback," she confessed. "That night."

"Before you came to me, or after?"

"Does it matter?"

"I want to know how much I should punish myself for not kicking in your door."

"After," she admitted, letting her eyes cruise up to his face, linger on his lips. "I don't remember everything. It was like a warning. I just know that I can't talk about him."

"Him?"

"My brother."

"Uriah."

"Yeah." Hannah nodded ever so slightly as Liam's eyebrow raised in question.

"That's funny," he said. "He's the only thing Flynn won't talk about either."

He wanted to kiss her. Hell, he wanted to pin her up against the wall and remind her what he could do to her... what he could make her feel. But she didn't want that. No, in fact, she regretted giving herself to him at all. And there was no *way* he was going to beg.

It didn't matter how much that truth made him to want to hike out of the compound and never look back. Despite the pain tightening his chest, Liam wasn't going to run from her; not when Hannah still needed him, even if she didn't know how to ask.

"When we leave this cabin, we're going back to the stone house and you're going to do exactly what I say."

Hannah nodded, her golden hair shimmering just a little in the firelight. Perspiration had gathered on her brow and she swiped at it with the sleeve of her heavy jacket.

She was nervous. Whatever was going on with Uriah

was big. The little redhead had been adamant about it, too. She would discuss everything, in front of everyone, as long as it didn't involve Hannah's brother. He was off limits.

The interrogator inside of him pushed Liam to seek out information about Uriah by any means necessary. If he had been dealing with soldiers or even other men, there would have been no question as to his methods.

But instead, he found himself juggling three women. One of which teetered on the edge of sanity and another that could end him with a single touch. Liam only ever felt equal to Flynn, but she still needed a soft hand and plenty of maneuvering. If he was being honest, this sort of political tap dance was more Cole's speed. But his friend was in over his head with the team, so it was up to Liam to balance this one out.

"Whatever happens, you are going to nod and agree with me." Liam lifted his hand to tilt Hannah's chin up. He wanted to look into her eyes, to make sure she understood what he was saying. "Flynn's not going to like what you have to say about Andy. She's not going to want to hear the truth, but you're going to tell her. All of it."

"But-"

"Don't sugar coat it." Liam let his thumb play along her jaw line, that stubborn, beautiful jaw line. The one he no longer had a right to touch. "But don't give her everything at once either. You've got to get as much from her as you can first. Can you do that?"

"I think so."

"Good." Liam retracted his hand to his side. "I'll do the negotiating."

Before she could answer, he turned on his heel and grabbed for his jacket. When he opened the door, Lena leapt to her feet, the collection of bedding still wrapped tightly around her small frame.

"You alright?" He asked.

"Yeah," her answer was as soft as she was.

Liam helped unwind her from the blankets before moving to toss them on the bed. He only broke stride for a moment when Hannah pushed past him in the dark. Damn it, he wanted her to wait for him.

Shrugging quickly into his jacket, he pulled the chair back through the front door and snapped it closed. Gritting his teeth, Liam made an effort to keep his hands loose at his sides. Lena would follow him regardless, so he didn't have to look back and check.

After a few paces through the trees, he spied Hannah standing still in the path, waiting. His heart jumped and the frown that had deepened his brow instantly relaxed. Good, he thought. They should walk back through the door of the stone house together.

Liam placed his boots deliberately, angling his head in order to watch Hannah's figure as she started hiking just ahead of him. It was late out, way past sunset and nearly impossible to see with the low layer of clouds.

Hannah was just visible in the glint of moon before it became hidden once more. The wind swept her hair, tangling it over her shoulders. They hadn't had fresh snow in weeks so the ground beneath their feet had been reduced to dirt. The temperature on the mountain hadn't been quite cold enough for it.

Liam inhaled now, testing the moisture hanging in the air. Would it turn into rain? He couldn't quite say.

When they reached the stone house, light from the fire and candles glowed through the glass windows. Hannah hesitated in front of the door, her hand poised to open it. Glancing back, those doe-brown eyes sought him out, causing Liam's chest to expand and contract once more. How long would she hold this power over him? Would he ever be free of it?

Giving his head a shake, Liam stopped just beside her and replaced her hand with his own. He would be the one to open the door. After all, he was running the show. It was important that they all be aware of it.

Looking over his shoulder, he confirmed that Lena was where she always was, behind him. Her breath panted out a bit, the brisk hike up the hillside still caused her a touch of strain. She needed to eat more, he thought.

On the other side of the door, voices murmured. You could hear the male undertones rippling, but the noise disappeared the second Liam opened the door.

As he stepped over the threshold, all eyes swiveled to meet him, all mouths closed in anticipation. Now here comes the balancing act, Liam thought, suppressing a smile. To all of them, he should look properly pissed at the level of compromising he was having to do. He wouldn't want them to think he had gone soft.

Clearing his throat, Liam stepped to one side and waited for Hannah and Lena to cross into the room. Once they had, he snapped the door closed and flipped its lock. He could appreciate the sound of the metal twisting against the wood, after all, he had made the mechanism himself.

"Bring two chairs over to the fire," Liam instructed. "Flynn and Hannah will be talking tonight, but I have a few ground rules."

Cole's eyes shot to him, and a general grumbling rose in the room. Liam avoided his friend's look, though he knew that would be hard on Cole. In this sort of dance, appearances are everything, and he didn't want the team to think he was doing Cole any favors. Which of course, he was.

Every person in here would be getting a little bit of what they asked for, but the most important aspect was that Cole didn't lose face. Cole had said he had to be in the room while Hannah and Flynn talked or nothing at all... and those were words Liam intended to stick by.

"First rule," Liam announced, raising his voice only slightly. "Consider yourself a guest at my party. If you're good, you get to stay and listen. If you piss me off... you're out on your ass."

Liam pointed to the front door, the one he had just locked, and let his eyes travel languidly over the crowd. They were quiet, that was good.

"Second rule," Liam continued. "There will be no commenting, talking, standing or touching... in fact don't fucking move at all. Just sit in your seat and keep your mouth shut."

Pausing, Liam watched the team shuffle about, trying to find a place to sit. Sure, half of them rolled their eyes but the other half swallowed nervously. At this point, he could give a shit either way.

Hannah and Flynn both made their way to the two wooden chairs by the fire. They were angled towards one another, though neither woman was willing to hold eye contact for long. That would change, Liam knew, and quickly.

"Third rule," Liam went on. "These two women have agreed to speak to one another with all of you present; however, they will not be discussing Hannah's brother, Uriah. This is a non-negotiable item so we'll just have to take what we can get."

The room stayed silent as the information rolled over them. Thankfully, no one so much as whimpered. If they had, Liam would've been forced to toss them out just to prove a point. Which he did not want to do. They all needed to be here. They all needed to see this.

Glancing down, he assessed the trembling bundle of nerves that shook by his side. Poor Lena, he hadn't been sure about her part in all of this, but she had agreed to it anyway. She had a strength to her still, even though she was fractured on the inside. Given enough time, he knew she would come out of the hell she continued to live in. Liam would give her all of the help that he could.

"You still sure?" Liam lowered himself to whisper.

"I am," Lena responded, tipping her head up and straightening her spine.

"You can stop whenever you need to," Liam reminded her.

To that, she just nodded and walked to the center of the room. All eyes settled on her as she shrugged out of her jacket. Flynn leaned forward to take the material, folding it neatly across her lap.

It was hot from so many bodies all pushed together for hours on end. Even Hannah began to work her coat loose now, letting it drape down over the back of her chair. Liam let his gaze find Chan, who stared at Lena, his jaw clenching.

"Chan-" Liam motioned for the other man to stand up. "I'm going to need you on this one."

Chan managed to tear his eyes away from Lena long enough to give Liam a rare scowl, but eventually he stood. Crossing to the table, Liam grabbed his knife from where he had left it and handed it over. Chan plucked at the handle and opened his mouth to speak, but before he could get a word out, Liam gestured to Lena.

She had rotated away from the men, hiking up her shirt to reveal the line of code that ran down her spine. In the firelight, you could see the hitch and shudder of her breathing. This may not work after all, Liam thought, but he pressed forward regardless.

"I need you to translate that code for us without touching her," Liam said. "Think you can manage it?"

Chan stared for a moment in silence, they all did. But

the ensuing quiet had a panicking effect on Lena. Her sides worked in and out, struggling to bring in enough oxygen. Liam tensed, feeling the weight of her standing exposed like this, with her back to seven men.

"The quicker the better," Liam hissed.

Gripping the knife firmly in hand, Chan crossed to where Lena stood and looked down at her back. He didn't reach out the way he had with Hannah, though Liam was sure he was tempted. Part of seeing the code printed like that seemed to be the need to run your fingers over it. If Chan felt the pull, he resisted.

Dropping to a crouch just behind her on the floor, he began scratching the marks into the planks of wood. Liam chanced a look at Cole who's eyes were riveted to Lena's back. No doubt he was already reading the gibberish for himself, he was the only other one who could.

"Some of you heard me ask Flynn about marks being placed on their bodies and now you can see what I was talking about," Liam began. "The answer to your next question… which you are *not* aloud to ask… is *yes*, Hannah and Flynn have them, too. And the next answer is, *no*, it wasn't any of your business until this moment."

Liam looked pointedly at Ace during this delivery and saw that he was right on point. The team had been rumbling about the marks since that first little fireside fiasco a few weeks back. None of them, with the exception of Cookie, had the guts to bring it to his face, though. Liam couldn't help but be pleasantly pleased by the notion. At least he still retained some manner of boundaries with the team, even if he seemed to have lost them completely amongst the women.

"All set," Chan announced and stood.

Exhaling a shaky breath, Lena pulled down her shirt and staggered forward. She covered her face with both hands before Flynn rose to meet her. The redhead wrapped her arms around the little china doll and whispered in her ear.

Shoving aside his twinge of guilt, Liam refocused on the task at hand.

"What's it say?"

"Female. Location 7. North America. Age at Year Zero: 20. Genetic Abnormalities: Present. Breeding: Sterilization. Name: Lena L. Francis. ID Number: 14337."

The rumbling that went around the room was instant and unavoidable. These stats were news to the majority of the team and the implications spoke volumes.

For Liam, Cole and Chan in particular it was the difference between Hannah's stats and Lena's that drew the most interest. But there was simply too much going on here to waste time guessing, which is why Liam had set up the rules in the first place. After a quick look to Cole, who raised his eyebrows, Liam stomped loudly towards the door.

"Rule Two!" Liam shouted, then unlocked the door and threw it wide. "No fucking talking!"

As he stood there facing them, letting the night air blow inside, Liam couldn't help but enjoy the flood of power he felt. Every single one of them fell silent.

Chan made his way back to his seat and Flynn released Lena to follow. After another beat, Liam closed the door and strode back to the center of the room.

"Can you explain the stats to us?" He asked. His question was aimed at Flynn, who actually blushed and squirmed a bit before speaking.

"When we arrived at the Wall, we went through a sort of processing." Flynn looked to Lena who folded in on herself. "It was still being built at the time, not the perimeter wall itself, but the insides. Not all of the apartments were finished, and most of the amenities were not fully operational. It takes time to build things, time to make them run properly and of course it takes man power.

That was why they collected skilled personnel that fell outside of the age and gender brackets. They needed engineers to design and tradesmen to construct. Because I'm a nurse, I was placed immediately. My job for the majority of the first two years was to conduct a physical examination of each new person."

Flynn turned her head to stare almost sadly at Hannah.

"You were my assistant. You helped me."

Hannah frowned at this information, her eyes dropping to her lap where she fidgeted with her fingers. Liam could feel the uncertainty roll off of her, she didn't want to believe it.

"As part of the exam we took DNA swabs, catalogued patient medical history, and placed IUD birth control in all females. You have to understand…" Flynn turned to Liam now, almost pleading. "It was mandatory, everything we did was required."

She's leaving something out, Liam realized, and debated whether now was a good time to press her for it. Before he could decide, Flynn turned back to Hannah, her hazel eyes darting over the other woman's reluctant face.

"You're a rich girl from Glencoe, Illinois. You went to private school and had the best of everything. You're dad was a high powered businessman who popped in and out of your life. He died when they bombed his office building. Your mom-"

"Stop." Hannah was shaking her head, her fingers jumping to massage her temples. "Stop. Stop!"

"You were nearly crushed to death in a prison panic but a soldier broke his wrist reaching through the bars to save you. Do you really not remember it?"

"Stop!"

"Do you really not remember the soldier?"

Hannah leapt to her feet. Her chair tipped back, clattering noisily to the floor. Squeezing her eyes shut, she kept shaking her head, her mouth moving.

Liam tensed, fighting against every instinct in his body that urged him to intervene. Whatever damage was being done, it was worth it. In this moment, Flynn was giving them more than she had intended, and they needed her raw and exposed like this.

Holding out a hand, Liam stopped any forward progress Cole wanted to make. Liam didn't have to look back to feel his friend rising from his chair.

"Because it was Andy," Flynn's voice was quiet. "He saved you that day."

"I don't remember him being there," Hannah offered, her voice ragged as she opened her eyes.

"What do you remember about him? What happened Hannah? Why didn't he come back for us?"

Hannah sucked in a breath and her eyes sought Liam. Now? She was asking him. Do I tell her now? And Liam gave his head the slightest shake. Not yet, sweetheart, not quite yet.

"Tell us about the genetics." Liam strode over to Hannah's chair and righted it. Staring all the while at Flynn, he motioned for Hannah to resume her seat. "Tell us about the breeding classification."

"And then it's her turn?" Flynn's eyes were red, she was on the verge of tears. "Then she tells me about Andy?"

"Then she tells you about Andy."

Flynn ducked her head and swiped at her eyes with the back of one hand. Liam noted that it trembled just a touch. When she looked up though, she seemed solid.

"DNA results take a long time to get back." Flynn had eyes only for Liam now. "Especially when you're processing thousands of people in an incomplete lab that is understaffed. For the first two years, when the screening would come in, the person would be notified and then get the laser stamp on their back. We didn't know what it all meant then. We were just trying to build a life. We were just trying to ride out the war."

"So what does it mean?"

"If your DNA comes back free of genetic markers for disease, then you're fine. You get a microchip implanted in your hand, and you move on with your life."

"And if it doesn't?"

"Then you're scheduled to be sterilized."

"Why?"

"So you can't pass your imperfect DNA on to the next generation."

"What are they trying to do? Create a master race?"

"No." Flynn huffed an ironic laugh. "They're curing the human race of illness. The microchip prevents you from getting sick due to the outside environment. No more flu, no more malaria, no viruses or bacterial infections."

"So, Hannah had the microchip because her DNA is what… pure?"

"Hannah has no genetic markers for disease. No cancer, no thyroid problems, no diabetes or heart disease. She was cleared for breeding. Lena and I were not."

"Is that why you left? Because they were going to sterilize you?"

"Yes," Flynn admitted, her cheeks pinking just a bit. "We got out before our appointments."

"Were there others?" Liam took a careful step closer. "Others that got out?"

"I've answered your questions." Flynn shut him down, her eyes popping back over to Hannah. "Now it's her turn."

CHAPTER SEVENTEEN_
COLE

He was breaking them... the women. Because that's what Liam did, he broke people. Cole swiveled his head to the right and took in Lena's hunched form. Perched next to Chan she had curled herself into the tiniest ball imaginable. Every so often, a tremor went through her.

As Cole watched, Chan leaned in close and whispered next to her ear. What he said was barely audible, but he repeated it over and over. *I'm sorry*, he said. *I'm so sorry.*

Squaring his shoulders, Cole turned his attention back to the two women at the center of the room. The fire had burned lower now since no one was allowed to move. Its dying flames licked at glowing logs, throwing ever increasing shadows into the corners.

On the wall behind him, Cole knew there was an old oil lamp still burning bright. They would need to add more of its meager fuel to their list of trade items. But what did it matter at this very moment? Why did Cole's mind work like that? Always absorbing and dancing from item to item, even when all the while other people's lives were unraveling around him.

Liam was the only one who stood now. His broad shoulders were taut, his hands clutching and un-clutching at his side.

Though the questioning style was different, this was still just an interrogation for him, Cole realized. This is just what he looked like when he carved soldiers into pieces. It was in the intensity with which he carried himself, the set of his jaw, the shift of his body. Like a lion stalking his prey, the energy was palpable.

Several times, Cole'd had to talk himself down from stopping the whole show. The way Hannah's face had gone from angry to vacant sent twists of unease up his spine. But the information they were getting, the things Flynn was saying, it caused a mix of shock and confusion. He needed more, much more.

"For the longest time, my earliest memory was of Andy yelling at me to run." Hannah cleared her throat, glancing from Liam to Flynn. "It wasn't until much later that I remembered him cutting the microchip out of my hand. I must have passed out or something and he had to drag me through the door of the Wall because we were both on the ground when I came to."

Hannah sucked in a breath, her hands shaking in her lap. Flynn's mouth was in a firm line and her eyes had stopped blinking.

"You have to understand," Hannah's voice took on a

pleading quality. "I didn't recognize him, I didn't even know my own name."

"You wanted to go with us," Flynn said. "You begged to go... for months. Andy was helping you."

"Yes," Hannah acknowledged. "Andy took care of me. I always did everything he said. I'm just trying to explain that... that..."

"That what?"

"That I only ever knew what he would tell me. I didn't know anything for myself."

"What are you trying to say? What happened when you guys came back for us?"

"That's the thing." Hannah hesitated, her eyes jumping to Liam, who only nodded. "We never went looking for you."

"What?" Flynn's face screwed up with the shock of it.

"He never mentioned you... or Lena."

"I just-" Flynn's mouth dropped, then snapped shut. She gave a quick shake of her head, then mumbled through gritted teeth. "This is unbelievable. Is that the story you've been telling your boyfriend?"

"It's true-"

"Then how did you all find us? Huh? How did you know where we were at? You left us there for months! You and Andy! How could you?"

Flynn shot to her feet, her hands raking desperately through her hair. Pacing back and forth, she refused to look at Hannah who rushed on, trying to explain the unexplainable. The truth was, only Cole and Liam knew that

Andy had purposefully traded his own girlfriend for a couple of sleeping bags and a fucking gun. They hadn't told anyone else, not yet.

"We traveled around all the time." Hannah's head tracked Flynn's movements, her eyes never leaving the other woman. "He had no destination in mind. If there was a goal or a point to any of it, then he never told me."

"Bullshit!" Flynn whirled on Hannah, her eyes full of betrayal and pain.

"I only found you after he died. But I was alone and afraid. I heard Lena crying. Once I saw the cage, I ran. I ran away from you, I'm so sorry." Tears leaked from Hannah's eyes.

The look on her face, it gutted him. Like she was the one responsible instead of that Andy asshole. Cole ground his teeth slowly inside his head, gripping his wooden chair reflexively with his fingers.

"I don't believe you," Flynn croaked.

"It's true."

"Why would he do that? How did he die? What the hell did you do to make him leave us like that?"

"I didn't do anything!" Hannah's hands went up, palms out. "He got shot in the head by a group of men. He had crossed a river and I was still swimming when they found him."

"No."

"They made him kneel on the bank-"

"No!"

"And they killed him right there."

"You're lying!"

"I'm not!"

"It doesn't make any sense!" Flynn stopped in her pacing, turning to face Hannah. "Why would he do that? Leave us and go back for you and then what? Just hike around for months? You did something to him, you convinced him to take you somewhere. You did meet with Uriah after all, didn't you?"

"He never mentioned Uriah." Hannah's eyes darted to Liam, then down to her lap. "And I'm not going to either."

Cole's heart pounded in his chest as he caught the quick glance Liam threw him over his shoulder. So this was the reason for all the maneuvering. Hannah's brother. He was a critical piece of this puzzle. So critical, in fact, that Hannah had lied to Cole about it.

She remembered more, more than she was willing to say. Damn, but that hurt. Had she told Liam? Cole's face flushed with the thought of it.

"Screw you, Hannah," Flynn seethed. "You don't get to be self-righteous with me. You think I'm going to destroy everything because of you? Don't flatter yourself."

"I did what Andy told me to!" Hannah leapt to her feet now, a red heat coloring her cheeks. "He's the one who led me inside the perimeter wall. He's the one who wanted to cut out the chip. I didn't want him to but he forced me anyway. He… he held me down and dug it out of my hand with his knife while I screamed. I can still taste his palm covering my mouth."

"You always wanted to come with us," Flynn cut in.

"You begged to get that chip out of your hand. You couldn't stand being left behind."

"I'm sure that's true." Hannah was panting now, a whine creeping into her voice. "But all I remember is telling him no. Then after… I woke up with a big blank page in my brain and I did exactly what Andy told me to. I only ever did what he said."

"Tell her, Hannah." Liam took a prowling step forward, nodding towards Flynn. "She deserves to know."

"No." Hannah shook her head, her pleading eyes darting to hold on Liam before whispering, "Please."

"Tell me what?" Flynn folded her arms across her chest.

Hannah's head dropped to her hands. Covering her face, she sat heavily back in her seat. The sound of her sucked in breath shot a dose of adrenaline right through Cole.

Enough of this shit, he thought, enough. Shoving up to standing, he began to walk forward when Liam shifted. It was like his old friend could sense his every move, blocking his path decidedly without having to look back. Before Cole could even extend his hand, Liam was already out with it.

"Andy told Hannah they were married," Liam stated. "And it wasn't just words, either. He made her his wife in every way that he possibly could."

Silence. One, beat, then two.

Flynn's face flushed with denial before morphing into anger. The rage that rushed from her body was palpable.

Lunging forward, Flynn threw herself at Hannah, a cry of anguish and outrage ripping from her throat.

Then it was like everyone was moving and yelling and swirling all at once. Hannah tipped back in her chair, her arms flying out in a vain attempt to save herself. Flynn landed on top of her. They were both on the ground. Then it was Liam and Cole and Ace piling on, all struggling to intervene.

By the time Ace and Cole hauled Flynn up, the sassy, unbreakable redhead was sobbing like a baby. Eyes tracking, Cole watched Liam drag Hannah into his arms before carrying her out the front door and into the night. She was pounding her little fists on his chest, shaking her head, her eyes squeezed shut against the reality that played out before them.

"You got her?" Cole looked to Ace who simply nodded.

Releasing his grip on Flynn, Cole jogged to follow Liam out the door. Once he breached the threshold, the cold wind swept over him and he slammed the wooden door shut with a decided snap. Eyes adjusting to the darkness, Cole followed the sound of Hannah's small voice. They were just a few yards away and he moved fast to meet them.

"She never had to know," Hannah was moaning the words, her body being held up only by the strength of Liam's grip on her arms.

"Andy was a bastard," Liam replied. "She needed to know the truth about him, otherwise her loyalty would always be with him. She needed to know how he betrayed her."

"What does it matter?" Hannah looked up into Liam's face. "He's dead now."

"The truth matters." Liam didn't break eye contact with her, but the shift in his stance told Cole he knew he had joined them. "Who you trust matters."

"You didn't have to do it like that, in front of everyone."

"Why?" Liam asked. "Would you prefer a more private audience for your confession?"

Cole placed a hand between them. "That's enough, Lee."

"Don't you get it?" Liam's eyes were trained on Hannah, searching, desperate almost. "I'm going to go right back in there and Flynn is going to give me everything I ask for. You may think I'm a cold-hearted prick but I never do anything that isn't absolutely necessary. I would never betray you like Andy did. Even if you don't want to be with me anymore, you can always trust me."

Cole's eyes widened at Liam's declaration as Hannah struggled in his grasp. In the next second, Cole was pushing Liam back, stepping in to loop an arm around Hannah's waist. She didn't want to be with Liam anymore?

Hannah swayed and Cole had to steady her as tears poured down her cheeks. Shakily, she raised an accusing finger to point at Liam. She moved her mouth, but no sound came out.

Glancing over his shoulder, Cole saw the look of pure torture covering his friend's face. But in the next second, Liam was whirling away. He took three massive strides towards the stone house, his fist cocked back, all anger and frustration. He only stopped at the last moment, just short of putting his hand through the front window.

Without looking back, Liam jerked open the heavy door and stepped back inside.

"I never said that," Hannah whispered, collapsing against Cole. "I never said that to him."

"Shhh," Cole hushed her, stroking his hand down her hair, a knot of dread causing his stomach to drop. "Let's just go."

Nodding, she let him loop her arm over his shoulder and lead her down the hillside. The moon was completely covered now and the ground was difficult to see. For the most part, Cole guided them by memory, avoiding the occasional tree trunk that would swoop up tall before them. Hannah leaned an exhausted head on his shoulder, forcing him to bend awkwardly down to accommodate their height difference. He may not be as tall as Liam, but he still had a good six inches on her.

When they got to his cabin it was freezing cold and dark. The fire Cole had left burning that morning had snuffed itself out hours ago. Releasing Hannah to sit on the bed, Cole fumbled blindly for the box of tinder bundles he kept pushed up against the far wall. He hadn't had time to grab their jackets in their rush to get out of there. In just a shirt and pants, his body began to shake.

"Get under the covers," Cole called.

Searching in his pocket, he brought out a piece of flint and his knife. At first, he struck at it lamely. The chill that seeped into his bones caused him to glance a half-hearted blow that barely jumped a spark. The next time he didn't miss.

Bending forward, he puffed oxygen at the bundle until the smell of smoke rolled forth, causing him to choke and sit back. His hand moved sideways along the worn wooden floor until he grasped one remaining log. Damn it, he had forgotten to haul in more wood.

Jumping up, Cole made a dash outside and circled around his cabin to where the eaves overhung the ground. His pile of firewood was dwindling low but he still had a enough stacked to last another few nights. Grumbling under his breath, Cole grabbed an armful of the frozen logs and let himself back inside.

By the time he was done tending the flames, his entire body was trembling. He told himself he was only trying to shake himself warm, but there was more to it than that. Shedding his clothes, Cole hurried to slide under the covers next to Hannah. As he wrapped his arms around her, he noted she was still fully clothed and shivering.

"Let's take these off," Cole murmured, reaching to draw her shirt over her head.

"It's too cold."

"Let my skin warm yours."

Cole's fingers worked to undo the zipper of her jeans before sliding them down past her hips and away. Drawing her in close, he held her body flush against his, settling his chin over the top of her head.

For several moments, they lay in silence. His heart

beating hard. His stomach twisting with uncertainty. He could feel the warm draw of her breath as she exhaled into his chest.

"You're keeping something from me." Cole pressed a soft kiss to her hair. "Something about your brother."

"Cole-"

"It's okay." He squeezed her in tighter to him, trying to comfort himself with her continued presence. She was done with Liam. How much longer until she was done with him? "Have you told Liam?"

"Not everything," she admitted, and he could feel her nibbling at her lip.

The gesture had him softening, though all the while his heart thumped. A strange sort of fear was creeping up on him, wrapping its tentacles around him, flooding his blood stream with its poison. He couldn't believe what he was about to say. But the fact remained that it was the right thing to do. He had to offer, even if his whole body wanted to explode at the outcome.

"You don't want to be with Liam anymore," Cole began.

"I never said that."

"Does that mean you don't want to be with me either?" Cole's voice had gone quiet in his struggle to maintain control. "Are you going to leave me?"

"What? Cole-"

"Because I'll still help you," Cole rushed on, not ready to hear her answer, not ready to experience what he had seen on Liam's face. "You can live here, I'll move out."

"No-"

"It's not safe for you to travel." Cole held her still as she tried to shift. "You don't have to sleep with any of us to stay here. I promise-"

"Stop."

Hannah wriggled in his arms and after a beat Cole made himself let go. Holy shit he wanted to die right now. His chest had gone tight, he couldn't hardly suck in any air. But then she was kissing him, pressing her lips to his and suddenly he felt that his heart really was going to burst. Why was this all so fucking painful?

"I love you, Cole," Hannah whispered to him, laying her forehead carefully against his. "I don't want to leave you."

"But you don't trust me," Cole stammered. "You tell Liam more than me, and you don't even love him."

"I never said I didn't love Liam."

"Then why don't you want to be with him anymore?"

"Because it's wrong," Hannah's voice was strained. "It's wrong for one woman to love two men. Don't tell me it doesn't hurt you."

Cole pursed his lips, exhaled through his nostrils. "It does," he admitted, although he said the words before he really had time to think it through.

Of course it hurt that she had been with Liam. But it hurt way worse thinking she might not want Cole anymore, either. And as far as right and wrong? Fuck. Those terms had been blurred and stretched and smashed until they no longer existed.

The war took everything from them. It took their homes, their friends and family. But it didn't stop there. It took their humanity and the rules by which they had once lived.

Cole reached up to touch Hannah's face, feeling the glisten of tears painting her cheeks. Hadn't they all been hurt enough? When would the suffering end?

"But I don't want to lose you," Cole amended, wiping at the wetness with his thumb. "I could get used to anything if it meant keeping you… if it meant you were happy."

"It's too much…"

"I'm going to stay out of it," Cole cut in. "This thing between you and Liam, I'm not getting involved. But I just want you to know that I support you, and someday maybe you'll be able to trust me with everything. Okay?"

"Okay." Hannah sucked in a breath and nodded.

When she nibbled on her lip, Cole couldn't help himself. Leaning closer, he covered her mouth with his own. She was so soft and her immediate acceptance of him sent a flood of warm relief through his body.

The muscles of his back relaxed as Hannah returned his kiss, giving as much as she was getting. This woman, there was something about this woman that did him in.

Letting loose a groan, Cole rolled on top of her and let his weight push her down into the mattress. Already naked, her warm body wriggled and arched against his own. He could feel the brush of her nipples on his chest, the wrap of her legs around his waist, the press of her heels against the small of his back.

It wasn't long before she had him battling with himself. *Slower, Cole. Slower.* He kept repeating the words over in his mind, but then she was tracing her tongue up his neck, sucking his earlobe into her mouth and he lost it.

Ducking his head, he let his tongue dance over each breast as he cupped and squeezed in turn. A little gasping cry escaped Hannah's lips and his hand cruised down between her thighs, rubbing and circling before dipping.

He slipped a testing finger inside and found himself gasping along with her. The way she pushed against him, arching and encouraging. She wanted him. That was all that mattered, she wanted him.

"Cole, please," Hannah panted.

"Say it again."

"Cole, I need you."

It was the words, in the end, that caused him to snap. Because the next thing he knew he was pushing himself inside of her. She cried out, clutching at his back, scraping her nails along his skin as he took what he wanted.

Over and over he rocked against her, marking her as his, pulling out and pushing in. The sensation dominated him, making him blind to everything. Squeezing his eyes shut, he buried his face in her neck and groaned. He couldn't keep this up much longer, he couldn't stop what was coming.

Faster and faster he went, tilting his hips forward, grinding against her, trying to give her the contact she needed. But then all he could hear was the sound of her moaning and he was up and over the edge, just barely able to take her with him.

When he collapsed down on top of her, he was dizzy. His breathing was ragged.

Blinking back into awareness, he could feel her body still pulsing around him. With a smile creasing his lips, he knew she had finished, too. And it was a good thing, because within a minute, he was out.

IT TOOK HIM LONGER THAN HE WANTED TO COLLECT himself. Standing just inside the door, Liam surveyed the fallout that resulted from being a monster. And that's exactly what he was, right? That's what Hannah saw when she looked at him, and she wasn't wrong.

Flynn was seated at the long wooden table, her forehead pressed against its flat surface, her arms outstretched before her. Ace was beside her, his hand rubbing slow circles on her back, his lips moving close to her ear. Every now and then, her body would arch with a sob, but then she quickly quieted.

Pacing the room in the corner, Davey glanced up when Liam began to move forward. Arms folded across his chest, brows furrowed, there was no mistaking the glint in the other man's eye. He would step in to protect the woman who had saved his brother's life.

Davey would do everything he could to stop what Liam

was about to do. Too bad for him, Liam thought, rolling his shoulders. Davey didn't stand a chance.

Liam hadn't come all this way to stop now. He hadn't sacrificed Lena's dignity and Hannah's perception of him to fall short. No, no. *That* was not going to happen.

"Rule two." Liam held up two fingers in Davey's direction as he took a seat opposite Flynn.

"Screw you," Davey spat, and had Ace lifting his head. "This stops now."

"How many soldiers live inside the Wall?" Liam asked, but Flynn only shook her head.

"Stop." Davey gritted his teeth.

"How many Flynn?" Liam ignored him, keeping his voice focused, but even. "Andy betrayed you. He was a piece of shit who fed you to the wolves. He didn't deserve you. He didn't deserve to draw another breath and now he's not."

"I can't believe it," Flynn choked out, turning her head to the side, her eyes squeezed shut.

"She's not answering your questions right now," Davey stepped closer. "You're taking advantage of her."

"No fucking talking!" Liam slammed his fist on the table, causing Flynn to sit up in surprise and Ace to tense. "If you say one more word I'm going to walk into the bunk room and start removing Ryder's stitches."

Davey's chin dropped and a flash of outrage flooded his face. But just beneath that, there was a layer of fear. He thought Liam might actually do it; like he might actually lay his hands on the kid. Another proof positive that Liam *was* in fact a monster. And it was no wonder.

Before Davey could speak, Liam held up a finger, wagging it back and forth.

"Ah, ah, ah," Liam said. "Not another word. In fact, you better go sit by his bedside, just in case."

Huffing out a breath, Davey pulled a hand down over his mouth and turned to stalk away. He would do as he was told, Liam knew. That was what made Davey such a good soldier. He had the ability to keep his mouth shut and follow instructions, even when everything inside of him told him that it was wrong.

If Cole had been here, things might have played out differently. But he wasn't and that was good. This was Liam's show, and he had to run it his way. None of the others could possibly understand.

Dropping his eyes back to Flynn, Liam noted she was staring at him soberly. What he had said served two purposes. Settle Davey's ass back down, and get her undivided attention. Perfect. Goal reached. Level unlocked.

"How many soldiers live behind the Wall?" Again, Liam's voice was remarkably calm.

"About five thousand." Flynn glanced down, her fingers were shaking as she stretched out her hands to watch.

"What types of weapons do they have?"

"They have guns, you know, like you all have."

"Rifles?"

"Yes."

"Anything heavier? Tanks, airplanes, helicopters, ground to air missiles, anything?"

"There's a bunker." Flynn glanced to the side at Ace. "I've never seen what's inside."

"Who runs everything?"

"Um…" Flynn dropped her eyes and gave her head a slight shake.

"Is there a government? Elected officials? Anyone from before?"

"No."

"So who calls the shots? Who's making you get sterilized? Who solves disputes?"

"I don't know."

"You don't know."

Flynn sucked in a ragged breath and slowly let it back out. Her hands fluttered, not seeming to be able to find their correct location. She folded them in her lap, propped them up on the table, then tucked her hair behind both ears. The nervousness was clear.

Liam chanced a look around the room and spotted Lena. She wasn't listening. She was beyond listening. Chan had her, though. He was sitting on the floor right beside her while she sat cross-legged near the fire, watching the flames. Someone had put on another log while Liam was outside.

A ripple of guilt threatened to distract him, but he shoved it roughly aside. She'd survive.

"Before now you couldn't tell the difference between a good man and a bad one," Liam stated, then watched Ace cringe at Flynn's expression. "But I think you can tell now, can't you? You've spent enough time with bad men to recognize what's around you. Look at Ace."

Flynn lifted her eyes and tilted her face to the side just a hair. She let her gaze flow over the medic, who sat very still, letting her access him. Of all people, Ace is the one she spent the most time with. They had even argued occasionally, but still seemed close. When Flynn returned her eyes to Liam, he knew he had her.

"We would get mandates from a source, they're delivered electronically. Do you remember having a pager? Were you old enough?"

"Yes," Liam nodded.

"Everyone has something like a pager, only you can text the source with issues and you receive decisions."

"So you do what it says."

"The soldiers enforce the mandates. Everyone follows the law, it's the law."

"Everyone just calls it the source? Who is it?"

"I couldn't say," Flynn shrugged. "I never met him."

"The marks on Hannah's back were a little different." Liam worked hard to keep the urgency from his voice. It was dangerous to let your subject know which questions meant the most to you. Keeping his breathing even and his face relaxed, Liam watched Flynn closely. "She had a breeding phase number. What is that?"

"Well, like I said before, her DNA came back free of disease markers. She was slated to have a baby."

"Slated. Give me more."

"The war nearly wiped out the human population." Flynn's eyes popped up to lock with Liam's. "Every genetically cleared female is required to reproduce, it was a mandate."

"A forced pregnancy?"

"Sort of." Flynn squirmed uncomfortably. "They were still screening the men when we left so nothing had actually happened yet."

"What was the mandate? What was the protocol supposed to be?"

"You could apply to pair with another person, but you had to be approved and pass the screening."

"What if you were denied? Or, what if you didn't want to be paired with someone?"

"Then you would be artificially inseminated with a match chosen by the source."

"And if you refused?"

"You were only required to have two babies. Any more was up to the woman."

"And if you wanted none?"

"Then you would be sedated..." Flynn looked away. "For the duration of your pregnancy, and someone else would raise the baby."

Ace leaned back and let a low whistle escape him. Glancing up, Liam noted that both Cookie and Trey were listening as well. Their expressions mirrored what Liam himself was thinking.

Who the fuck had enough money, enough power, enough resources to put all this together? In the midst of a world war, with all the chaos and the destruction, this sort of setup took a lot of careful planning and thought.

Not only that, but the execution of said plan and continued control over the new population would be an ongoing challenge. But why? What did it all mean?

"I'm assuming there are others like yourself that want to get out." Liam leaned forward, hands pressed together just beneath his chin. "It can't be just you, Lena and Hannah."

"It's not," Flynn admitted, refusing to meet his gaze. "But wanting to get out and actually getting out are two very different things. There are cameras everywhere, in all the homes and halls. Outside and inside, at work, at the cafeteria, in the parks. The source watches and listens to everything. The source knows everything. You can't step out of line even an inch and not get a text about it."

"What happens when you get a text? What happens when you're in trouble?"

"You forfeit your rations at first. No new clothes, less food, extra work shifts."

"And then?"

"They have a jail." Flynn cleared her throat and lifted her chin, but her eyes remained on the table.

"I get why you and Lena wanted to leave." Liam eased back, trying to give Flynn the appearance of space. "But why did Hannah want to go? What were they going to do to her?"

"You'll have to ask Hannah that."

Flynn's hazel eyes shot up to Liam's and flashed in

challenge. This was the beginning of the end, he could feel her slipping away from him, gaining back her former strength.

"She doesn't remember."

"Oh, really?" Flynn's eyebrows lifted. "You sure about that?"

Liam kept his face impassive, even let a small smirk tug at the corner of his mouth. On the outside, he gave every appearance of unruffled calculation. This was a chess match after all, and he had won… for the most part.

But inside, his gut clenched at the suggestion. He knew Hannah was holding back, she had admitted as much. But just how much? *That* he did not know.

And the fact fucking stabbed at him. Stabbed him in places he didn't know could hurt; right there in the center of his chest, where his cold dark heart still pumped with bright red blood.

"Fair enough." Liam blinked at her. "How did you get out? If it was so hard, then how did you all manage it? Sounds like Andy was able to go back and forth."

"Andy." Flynn's face contorted as she choked on the word. "I'm done here."

Shoving up to standing, Flynn fought against the tears that rolled down her face. Despite her anger, she couldn't stop the flow. For a split second, Ace's eyes darted between the redhead and Liam.

It wasn't until Liam folded his arms across his chest and looked away that Ace stood up and moved to help her. Liam knew he had a better chance at getting more later if he let her walk away now. The interrogation was finally over.

At this point, another man may have said he was sorry. Another man may have regretted the trauma he brought on with all of his threats and rough questioning. But Liam felt no remorse whatsoever. He was already planning his next attack.

And it was this lack of humanity that was his fatal flaw, his tainted bloodline, his inheritance so to speak. He let the others step in and comfort where he had nothing left to give. In the end, you couldn't be truly good at this sort of thing if you tolerated even an ounce of sympathy.

That was one lesson he learned too well from his fucking father. If you're going to do something, better go all the way.

"Can we go?" Lena's voice came out beside him, soft as a lullaby.

Jerking his head up, Liam squinted at the slight woman who held herself straight before him. Just behind her figure, Chan shifted his weight from one foot to the other. It was only for a split second, but Liam caught the look of intense concern that riddled Chan's face. Then it was gone, wiped clean by force of habit.

Hmm. There was something more here, Liam thought briefly, but then his brain was flashing elsewhere.

"You still want to go home with me?" Liam asked.

Lena simply bobbed her head and swallowed. Her tiny hands were clasped calmly in front of her and she had donned her heavy coat already. A thousand questions darted through Liam's mind. Wouldn't you feel more comfortable staying here with Flynn? Or even going back to Chan's place? Didn't you see what I just did to your friend? What I did to Hannah, and even to you?

But Liam didn't have the luxury of asking these things aloud. He was the big bad wolf here, all confidence and surety. You couldn't convince people to bare their soul to a room full of people one minute and then spout insecurities the next.

"Alright, then." Liam spread his palms on the tabletop and pushed slowly to his feet. "Let me grab my jacket."

BACK OUTSIDE IT WAS BLACK AS PITCH. LIAM WASN'T SURE what time it was but he judged that dawn would probably come in another hour or possibly less. The slope to his cabin was steep but flanked by thick trees. He could pick his way by feel, occasionally reaching out to guide himself with a hand against a trunk. Lena, on the other hand, was struggling.

He could hear her stumbling steps, her huff of surprised breath as she tried to keep up. She was so much smaller than he was, she couldn't reach from one tree to the next in the night.

"Grab onto my jacket," Liam said.

Slowing his body until he felt her just behind him, Liam waited for her to clutch at his back. He nearly jumped out of his skin when she took his hand instead. The contact was unexpected to say the least.

Clearing his throat, he slipped his hand from hers and placed her fingers on the material where he had instructed. She didn't resist or say anything, so he started forward, but at a much slower pace.

All at once, it hit him. The weight of the past few days settled itself on the back of his neck, pushing down. By the time they breached his front door, Liam's head was throbbing.

Thankfully, it was still fairly warm inside. The fire he had kept roaring while dragging the women in and out for questioning had burned low, but it still burned.

Absently, he shoved one more log into the grate before adjusting the air vent. Lena was already under the covers on the bed when he turned around. Wriggling out of her clothes she changed into one of his shirts. It was giant on her, bigger even than a dress.

Stepping out of his boots, Liam rubbed at the base of his skull before shrugging out of his jacket. For the first time in a month, he really, really missed his mattress. His bedroll did well enough but the extra cushion would have been much appreciated just about now.

Oh well, he thought, he wasn't going to go back on his word. He would stay with Lena until she was ready to be on her own. Maybe if his mom had had the same option... well, fuck.

Shaking his head, he gritted his teeth and pushed his fingers hard against his closed eyes. No room for that.

Stooping down, Liam crawled into his sleeping bag, not bothering to take off his jeans or change his shirt. Sleep would come for him quickly, and then none of it would matter anymore.

The way Hannah had looked at him wouldn't matter. The fact that she didn't want him anymore wouldn't matter. His breath came slow and even, his muscles tensed and released. Just before the fog took him, he heard Lena speak.

"You asked why Hannah wanted to leave," she said, and had Liam's pulse kicking up uncomfortably.

"Yeah." He cleared his throat. Waited.

"Well, she was only Flynn's assistant for a year."

Lena paused then and it seemed the silence would go on forever. Liam's chest cinched tighter, his eyes popping open to watch the split wood logs of his ceiling.

But then suddenly her voice cracked the quiet once more. "She got transferred. She became the administrative assistant to the source."

"So, she saw him? She knows who he is?"

"Yes, he's the reason she wanted to leave."

"Why?"

"I don't know," Lena exhaled. "She refused to say."

CHAPTER NINETEEN_
LIAM

The ting of the hammer striking the anvil filled the air. Liam gritted his teeth, putting as much energy as he could into each swing. His canvas jacket lay discarded on the floor as sweat beads gathered on his brow. A damp V shape worked its way down the back of his shirt.

Though it was plenty cold in his shop, he didn't feel it. He didn't feel hardly anything when he worked like this and that's exactly how he liked it. This particular knife would be about twelve inches long when he was finished. At this point, it was coming along nicely.

Pausing for a moment, he lifted the blade to eye level and ran his thumb along the area he was working. Might need to heat it again, in order to really get the shape he was after. Flexing his hand, he had to smile at the calluses that had finally formed. Two weeks ago they were just budding blisters.

Although now that he thought about it, there was

something about the stinging pain and bloody palms that he sort of missed. But all in all it felt good to be back at work. In fact, it was the only time he actually felt that word anymore… *good*.

"You can't keep doing this," Chan's voice sounded from the threshold of the open door.

Liam huffed a dismissive breath, twisting his head to eye Chan a moment. The other man held a plate of food in one hand and a fresh bucket of water in the other.

"She needs to eat," Chan continued, knowing Liam wasn't about to answer. "You may be able to marathon like this but Lena can't handle it."

"If she gets hungry enough, she'll go get food," Liam reasoned, turning his attention back to the knife. He'd definitely have to re-heat it now.

"You're a thoughtless dick, you know that?" Chan spat. "I don't know what she sees in you."

Liam waved a hand absently over his head as Chan stomped the few feet to the cabin's front door and let himself inside. The truth of it was, Liam *had* been concerned about Lena. Especially when she refused to leave him, even to eat. He had hoped his strategy of waiting her out would work sooner. He had hoped she would get hungry enough to break away and learn first hand that she was safe without him.

After two days of starvation, however, Chan was forced to step in. He started bringing her every meal, and anything else she asked for, too. Little did Chan know, she fed Liam from the portions he brought. Of course Liam wasn't all that hungry these days, but every once in awhile her persistent nagging would get to him and he'd chew on a hunk of dried mutton just to shut her up.

What the others all saw as a self-absorbed addiction, Liam knew was the only thing saving him. He hadn't told any of them about what Lena had said. He hadn't even confronted Hannah about the extent of her memories, or the fact that she had worked for the source, whoever he was.

To Liam, it just didn't matter anymore. She didn't want him. Regretted sleeping with him. Fuck.

Seeing Hannah now was just too damn painful. The way her golden hair drifted over her shoulders in the wind, or the smile on her face when Cookie and she made meals together. It was like a vice clamped down on his chest. He couldn't stand it. Couldn't stand the slow suffocation of it.

So he'd been holed up in here for the past three weeks. Cowardly? Yeah. He could admit that much.

Reaching into the pocket of his jeans, Liam gripped her tiny bracelet, ran its cold links through his fingers. After those first few days together, those stolen days that haunted him, she had left it behind.

At the time she'd still been spouting rules about balance and respect. But she'd told him she would come back for it, that she would wear it every day that she belonged to him.

Only thing was, that last part never happened. She'd never come back to his bed. She'd never put it on again. At this point, if Liam didn't have the knife work to distract him, then he'd have already left, promise or no.

In the back of his mind, he knew it was just a waiting game now. All he needed was for Lena to be okay without him, then he could go. But she was taking so damn long and Chan wasn't helping matters. The urge to get the hell out of this place was coming on stronger every single day.

Bringing the knife up to his lips, Liam tapped slowly, thinking. Maybe he needed to switch up strategies.

Flipping the blade quickly in the palm of his hand, Liam strode out of his shop and into the small cabin. It was almost painfully hot inside. His forge was roaring, it'd been running practically non-stop. Lena was sitting cross-legged on the bed in nothing but a t-shirt, the window thrown open wide to let in the winter air.

A plate filled with food was balanced neatly on the edge of the mattress and her fragile fingers gripped a fork with which she speared a pancake. Must be breakfast, Liam thought. He didn't hardly keep track of the time anymore.

Chan was in the far corner, stooping to switch out the full water bucket for an empty one. Eyeing him, Liam noisily grabbed a few more logs and fed them to the fire. He would need it even hotter than this to get the metal molten. Did it disregard Lena's comfort? Hell yes it did.

Upon hearing him, Chan straightened, a sneer of disdain warping his once placid features. Over the past few weeks, Liam had been treated to a full display of Chan's slow but steady unraveling. The man who once held the all time poker win record for their team, now couldn't keep a single emotion private.

It had taken Liam three days of occasional observation

to finally figure out why. Another time in his life Liam would have chided himself at being such an idiot. If he hadn't been so damn distracted, he would've seen it much sooner. But alas, the truth was that Liam didn't hardly give a shit anymore... about anything. All that mattered was leaving.

"Mmmm." Liam forced a smile to his lips. "Looks good."

Lena's eyebrows shot up in surprise as he took a step towards the bed and grabbed a pancake for himself. Shoving the whole thing into his mouth, Liam did his best not to choke on the food before swallowing it down. The taste of it was abhorrent to him.

His stomach soured at the contact, but there was a purpose to his madness and so Liam kept up the show. If he didn't eat another bite of food in all his life, he didn't think he'd care.

When he finally got free of this place, he could let his body and mind war in peace. He wasn't sure which one would win really. Either his heart would have him starve to death, or his body would rally against it.

"You *feed* him?" Chan's voice was incredulous, his eyes accusing as his head whipped between them.

"Chan-" Lena began, but he cut her off.

"He would starve you... but you feed him."

Lena's face dropped and she scrambled to her knees, reaching out. Her fork clattered to her plate. Her big blue eyes filled with guilt.

Chan might have melted at her expression but he was too busy brushing past her to notice. Slamming through the front door, the soldier took one giant step before chucking the empty wooden bucket down the hill.

Just right, Liam thought, as he strode after Chan, careful to shut the door securely behind him. Wouldn't want little princess doll to overhear anything. She'd stay put, too, right where Liam left her. Because she knew he wouldn't truly leave her there. He would always remain within a few dozen feet, until she was ready, just like he promised.

"Do you know why she stays with me?" Liam lifted his voice, but not too loudly.

And of course Chan stopped dead in his tracks. All it took was a mention of Lena and he was done for. Liam almost felt sorry just then. *Almost*. He definitely understood that helpless feeling.

Shoulders heaving, hands clenching, Chan sucked in air for several moments before finally turning around.

"Because she likes assholes?" Chan's eyes were blazing as Liam closed the short distance between them.

"You're an asshole," Liam reasoned, his voice dropping to a whisper.

"Not like you."

"Just like me, Chan."

"Fuck. You."

Chan pushed the words out through clenched teeth. They had both done terrible shit. Bad, awful, deadly shit. And though Liam didn't know the specifics, something had gone down during that last mission. Something that Chan wasn't proud of.

So there was a weakness there, and Liam would exploit it. Liam could lie to himself and say it was only to benefit Lena, but what was the point in that? This whole charade was for one thing and one thing only... to get himself the hell out of here.

"She stays with me because I don't look at her with hungry fucking eyes." Liam watched Chan's face carefully, and he saw the second his little comment hit home. "She stays with me because she knows that I'm never, ever, going to crawl off that floor and into her bed."

Chan exhaled. His face shifting with shock, acceptance and then shame. But that last emotion wasn't one Liam was going for. No, there was no shame in wanting someone the way Chan wanted Lena.

He was no pushy, demanding prick. In fact, Liam judged him to be just right... patient. Really, really patient.

"Move in with us, Chan," Liam stated it. Commanded it. It wasn't a question.

"What? But you just..."

"That's why she chose me and that's why she stays," Liam tried to explain. He hated putting words on things. Especially things you just *know*. But in this instance, he had to try. "I'm like a brother to her. I'm only telling you so you don't get all fucking jealous and do something stupid. You can't screw this up."

"You want me to live in there." Chan gestured to the small cabin. "With both of you."

"Consider it a sort of transition," Liam supplied. "You're going to prove to her that you aren't going to crawl up off the floor either. You're going to wait and see if she comes down to you."

"I-"

"It could be years," Liam qualified, eyes darting over Chan's face. "Or never. She could live the rest of her life and never come down off that bed to you. How long could you stay on the floor?"

"Forever," the word leapt from Chan's mouth without hesitation. "I'll never get up off the floor."

"Great." Liam slapped Chan on the shoulder once... hard. "Go get your shit. And when you come back, don't bother me with your moody fucking attitude anymore."

CHAPTER TWENTY_
HANNAH

THE SOUND OF THE WATER RUNNING IN THE CREEK WAS worth it. Rippling and swirling, tripping along the banks on either side, the flow was constant, steady and sure. Hannah sucked in a breath and shoved her arms back into the freezing stream once more.

She'd shed her coat, rolling up the long sleeves of her button down shirt. Kneeling on the bank, she dipped the heavy blanket beneath the surface, then used all of her strength to fish it back out. The bar of soap lay beside her.

Dragging the sodden mass just far enough up on the bank, she began to work the suds in. Back and forth. She shoved the bar over the material until her shoulders ached and her knees protested the hard ground.

It was the dead of winter but Hannah didn't care. She liked the solitude. She liked the work.

"Don't you have a tub you can wash this in?" Cookie

came to crouch beside her, eyeing first the blanket, then Hannah's face.

"This one's too big for it," Hannah supplied, and it was the truth.

"It's maybe forty degrees out," Cookie continued. "Sunshine or no, it's not gonna dry out here."

"Then I'll haul it back to the cabin."

Cookie grunted, scratching at his bearded chin.

Focusing on the blanket before her, Hannah let her hair fall down to shield her face. She didn't need one of Cookie's little visits just now. If she thought there was a way to get rid of him without causing more trouble, then she'd do it.

But there's no way that was happening. She'd spent enough time with the older man by now. She knew. The best way to handle him was to give him nothing at all. Don't bite back. Don't tell him to get lost. Just be pleasant and boring.

That's right. Boring, pleasant Hannah, with the accepting face and the controlled disposition.

The moment the thoughts flashed through her mind, a bright pain stabbed at her temple. Ducking her head, Hannah couldn't help but gasp and press the back of her wrist to her head.

The headaches had started weeks ago, and they just wouldn't let up. They happened whenever she remembered something. They happened whenever something she thought about rang true from before.

Sometimes it was just a sentence and other times it was

an entire sequence of events. But the most painful aspect wasn't the accompanying throbbing in her head or the incessant thirst that plagued her after. The most painful part was how right about everything Flynn had been, so incredibly right.

Turns out Hannah *was* a worthless rich girl, complete with daddy issues and a therapist on speed dial. Though she still didn't have the full picture, she was getting more and more all the time.

Mostly they were memories from before the war. It made her miss her brother. It made her miss their mom.

"You okay?" Cookie was hunkered down beside her again, steadying her shoulder with one hand.

"I'm fine." Hannah huffed a laugh, trying to play it off.

"More headaches?"

Hannah flashed a fake smile at him before pulling away. Back on her feet, she dragged the soapy blanket back to the stream and shoved it beneath the water. She was still hiding her memories from the men, Cole included, but the headaches were just too obvious.

Behind her, Cookie rose to standing and stepped to one side, angling his body so that she could see him. Working hard to ignore the older man, Hannah held her breath against the cold, dunking the blanket in again and again. The water was rinsing everything clean, although her skin was paying an icy price.

"So, Chan's been living with Lena and Liam for a few weeks now," Cookie stated. "Seems like an odd arrangement, don't you think?"

Hannah simply shrugged and shoved her arms down further in the creek. What did she care what Liam did with his girlfriend? Of course her chest still constricted at the thought, but Cole had already mentioned it awhile back, so at least she didn't feel like crying anymore.

"You just gonna sit there and pretend?"

Hesitating for a moment, Hannah had to clear her throat before continuing on. That's exactly what she was going to do, pretend.

Clutching onto the heavy blanket, Hannah hefted it up in the air as she rose to standing. Without looking at Cookie, she began to wring out the sodden fabric in tiny tight twists over the water. The drops erupted from the material, making lovely splashing sounds as they hit the creek.

Pretending is what Hannah was best at, that's what her therapist had said. And why wouldn't she be? That's what her parents had trained her to do her whole life.

Sit quietly in class. Cross your legs. Keep your lips closed and your ears open. Don't raise your voice. Don't make a scene. Don't cause a fuss. Don't disagree.

Don't pick up that fork, use the other one. Don't frown, keep a smile on your face. You're so pretty when you smile.

Just nod your head now. That's a good girl.

Hannah grimaced, the scar on her hand throbbing now along with her head. She could go on and on and on.

"If it bothers you so bad, why don't you just tell him?"

"Tell him what?" Hannah glanced at Cookie before

carrying the blanket to a nearby bush and spreading it out to dry in the branches.

"Tell Liam how you feel about him."

"There's nothing to tell."

"Really?!" Cookie threw up his hands. "Damn, but youth sure is wasted on the young."

"What do you care?" Hannah spat, whirling to face him. "The reason for us being together is over. He's with Lena now and she'll keep him here. It's just what you wanted when you first chose him."

Crossing her arms over her chest, Hannah glared. Her shirt and pants were wet now. The color of her skin was shading towards blue from the time spent in the near freezing water.

"*You* chose him, too," Cookie reminded her.

"Yes, I did." Hannah dropped her head at that, and began rolling down her sleeves. "But he chose Lena, so it's over, okay? What more do you want from me?"

"He's leaving, Hannah."

"On the supply run to the city, I know."

"No." Cookie's tone shifted, causing Hannah to look up at him. "I don't think he's coming back from it."

"What? Did he say something to you?"

"No." Cookie shook his head. "But it's a feeling I get. You need to talk to him."

"And say what?"

"That you're crazy about him! That as much as he's been avoiding you, you've been avoiding him right back!"

"How can you say that?" Hannah's mouth dropped.

"Even you think one woman being with two men isn't right. You said so just now about Chan and Lena."

"Because those three don't fit!" Cookie rubbed a hand behind his neck, looking at times frustrated and bewildered. "You and Cole and Liam, though… It's like you're already some strange sort of family or something. It works. Don't ask me how it seems fitting, but it just does."

"You're the one who's crazy." Hannah's heart rate increased as she dashed to her jacket and scooped it up. "If my daddy were here-"

"Well, he ain't!" Cookie called. "He's dead, along with everyone else! Look around you Hannah Mae. That whole world and all of its rules is gone."

Retreating up the hillside, Hannah marched steadily away, refusing to look back. Though her breath hitched and burned in her lungs, she would be damned if she let a single solitary tear roll down her cheek. She was done with the crying. Absolutely done.

Shoving an arm into her coat, she stumbled a bit on the grassy slope but thankfully didn't go down. The knees of her jeans were already damp from her work by the creek, she didn't need them covered in mud as well. It was then she realized she'd forgotten the blanket in her haste to get out of there. *Oh well, you can go back for it later.*

At the crest of the rise, the pasture gate stood, swaying slightly with a gust of wind. Wrapping her arms around her body, Hannah shook her head and tried like hell to keep her nerves under control.

Cookie really was crazy. It had been his whispering that

started this whole thing in the first place. *His* murmuring about the guys leaving and Cole losing his status as leader and her continued safety at the compound.

But then she'd just jumped in with both feet, hadn't she? Volunteering herself as bait to maintain order. Well, now look at the mess she was wallowing around in. The not being able to sleep thing, and then the fact that Liam's face just consumed her mind.

She hadn't expected to feel anything for him. It was supposed to be a business arrangement. Like, hey I'll let you have sex with me and then you'll stay and protect me. But when Liam pressed his lips to hers that first time, it was over. It was as if he soaked inside her, under her skin, making her want him somehow.

She'd spent the better part of the last two months trying to rid herself of that exact feeling. So far... she'd been unable to accomplish it.

"Identify the emotion and then give yourself permission to feel it," Hannah muttered the words from her therapist under her breath.

Without thinking, she climbed up the rungs of the pasture gate. All it took was one more swift motion and she was touching down on the other side. She didn't even bother to swing it open and shut.

Moving steadily towards Cole's cabin, Hannah was distracted. In the back of her mind, she knew she was damp from the washing and needed to change, but those logical thoughts were background noise. They barely made a ripple compared to the internal war she was waging.

Who was she really? And why was she suddenly always so weak?

She wasn't sure if remembering the occasional therapy session was a good or a bad thing. At least before the memories, she had actually *liked* who she was. Sure her mind was a blank page, but she'd been a survivor, right? That's what Cookie had called her back then.

When Andy had died, Hannah had lived. When the other women had been captured, she'd gotten away, stayed safe. Hell, she even sent the team back to save them.

But now that her past was looming larger and larger each day, Hannah couldn't help but continually question herself. Was she the perfectly groomed, well-mannered socialite that her father wanted? The one so filled with constraint and weakness that she just as soon stay on the sidelines than make a mistake?

Or was she the woman from after the war? The one who hunted wolves and swam across rivers. The woman who held Cole at gunpoint while seriously considering shooting him.

Before she could make up her mind, Hannah met with the heavy wooden door to Cole's cabin and shoved inside. It was warm. The fire still simmered behind the grate but no one was around. Quickly, she stomped to the far dresser and sorted through her remaining clothes.

There was no doubt the impending supply run was needed. Cole had been talking about it for weeks. The city the guys would be heading to lay due south of here, about ten day's journey depending on the weather.

At first, Hannah had tried to weasel her way onto the trip. After all, she went with them to rescue Lena and Flynn. But no matter how hard she tried, every single one of the guys had answered her in the same way. Everytime. *No.*

This was different than heading north, where the others were more scattered and they needed her to help navigate. This time they would be passing suburbs, small towns, highways and larger groups of men. Lots and lots of other men. It wasn't worth the risk. So, begrudgingly, she was staying put.

Selecting a long sleeve green thermal and slightly dirty pants, Hannah changed into them and set her wet clothes to hang by the fire. Around here, you had to wear things over and over before you even considered washing them. It took a lot of effort, not to mention soap, to clean.

And soap wasn't a resource they were looking to waste. Nope. In fact, it was a resource they intended to barter. The team would be hauling down bars of soap, small sacks of corn flour, pickled vegetables and of course, Liam's knives.

Grabbing her brush off the dresser, Hannah ran it roughly through her hair before twisting the golden mass into a long braid. Liam. The sound of his work echoed constantly throughout the camp. How could she ever get over him with his non-stop hammering?

It was like he did it just to taunt her. *I'm here and happy, working away, enjoying my new girlfriend and life... without you. Because you were just a lay. Nothing more than that.*

"You have Cole, you've got no right to be jealous," Hannah muttered to herself, selecting a scrap of material to tie off her hair with.

And wasn't that the worst part of it? She loved Cole, too. She wanted Cole, too. It was sick. With a shake of her head, Hannah stepped back into her boots and jacket before pushing out the front door. She had to stop. Just. Stop.

Outside, the sun continued to glow brightly in the sky. It was a rare break in the weather which is why Hannah had chanced to wash in the creek in the first place. But Cookie was right, as he always was. The wind continued to blow cold and the air was crisp. That blanket wouldn't be dry by the time the sun waned.

A part of Hannah had known that and yet done it anyway.

Why? Because maybe deep down she had hoped Liam would make a visit to the pasture? Because maybe she wanted to catch him alone, or for him to catch her? Like before? No, Hannah shook her head again. Enough of this.

Angling her steps up into the trees, Hannah headed for the stone house. The path was easier now, Davey and Trey had spent the past month installing a series of steps using cut logs. Hannah hiked along the smoothed down dirt for several feet before stepping up to the next level and then the next and the next.

Winding through the trees it wasn't long before the swirl of smoke drifted beneath her nose. She was nearing her destination and the sound of voices carried to her on the air. In the clearing, Flynn and Lena were standing together, watching Ryder try to hit a pinecone with a long stick.

Hannah exhaled, a smile forming on her lips. He was doing so much better. The stitches had come out and his wounds were safely closed. Ace still wouldn't let him do a whole lot yet, but he was allowed to play this game.

Flynn called it croquet-golf and Hannah had witnessed several of the guys participate in the past. But right now, it was just the three of them. For a moment, they didn't realize Hannah was there.

Ryder lined up his stick to the general murmuring of the two women. After shooting them a warning look over his shoulder, he took a controlled swing, careful not to twist back too much. When he let go, the stick came down and he missed the pinecone entirely, swiping at the air with a great whooshing sound.

Lena squealed, one hand shooting up to cover her mouth while Flynn let loose a gratifying laugh. Ryder cursed roundly before stomping over and giving the pinecone a good kick. It tumbled and splintered against the ground.

Hannah smoothed her braid back over her shoulder. It was nice to hear Flynn like that, she realized. It was nice to hear her laugh and to see Lena smile.

The more she remembered, the more Hannah understood how close they'd all been at one time. She still only saw bits and pieces from their time living together, but the feelings were all lining up. It made her want to speak to both of them. Made her want to make amends… though she wasn't quite sure how.

Now when the two women looked up and spied her, their faces fell, each to its own brand of reserve. Flynn scowled and huffed a breath while Lena pursed her lips and looked down. So much for renewed friendship. Hannah sighed and walked away, through the door and into the stone house.

"I think we need to leave an extra guy here," Cole was saying.

He sat at the long table which was covered with the team's tradable goods. The others ranged around him, some sitting, some standing a few feet back.

"If we go out with less than our usual six, there's going to be questions," Ace countered.

A rumble of assent moved through the men as Hannah shed her jacket and hung it on a hook by the door. This sort of back and forth was typical for the team before departing. Once they were outside the compound, however, it was Cole's call or nothing at all.

"Ryder still can't climb the ladder for watch," Chan tossed his opinion over his shoulder, not bothering to turn away from his spot by the window. He stood stock still, looking out, watching.

"There hasn't been any sign of other men on our mountain for over a year now," Ace again. The debate continued.

Hannah glanced at Cole a moment, but he was too absorbed in the discussion to acknowledge her. His brow was furrowed and his mouth held itself in a firm line.

Though Hannah was sure he wanted to say something, he kept silent and listened instead.

Scanning the array of faces, Hannah's heart sank just a touch when she realized Liam wasn't in attendance. Ugh, why did she still feel this way? Crossing to the window, she stepped up beside Chan and looked out.

Lena and Flynn were standing with their backs to the stone house, arms linked, still watching Ryder. He was saying something, and the two of them shifted once more, a ripple of laughter peeling from Flynn's lips.

Hannah couldn't help her audible sigh. This would be her whole life for the next several weeks. It would be Chan and Ryder staying at the compound with the three women. No Cole. No Cookie. It was shaping up to be a pretty lonely time.

"Wave," Chan instructed and nudged her with his elbow.

With a slight jump, Hannah tuned back in and looked through the window. Lena had turned around and was lifting a tentative hand. Of course Flynn stayed facing the opposite way, forcefully resolute. But the little dark-haired pixie, at least, was giving them a small smile.

Hannah felt Chan raise his hand to the glass and so she did the same. Glancing sideways at him, she noticed his bright smile. He was happy, she realized, happier than she'd ever seen him. And the feeling was a sort of relief to Hannah. At least someone here was.

"Thank you," Hannah whispered, as soon as Lena returned to the game.

"She's been telling me things," Chan confided. "Maybe you two could talk sometime."

"I'd like that." Hannah nodded, gulping at the thought of what Lena must be saying.

Before Hannah got up the nerve to ask for more information, however, the front door to the stone house opened and Liam walked in. His long arms were loaded down with a collection of knives. Some were wrapped in cloth and others had their own leather sheaths. All eyes shot up to track him as he stalked towards the table and unloaded his goods.

"Wow, I know you've been working hard but this is more than I'd hoped for." Cole stood up and reached for a few of the knives.

"That should be enough to supply the compound for the next year or so," Liam said.

Taking a step back, he dusted absently at his hands before allowing himself a quick nod. He had a short beard now, hiding the skin of his chin and cheeks. Letting her eyes sweep over him, Hannah noticed a thinness to his face that wasn't there before... and he was a touch pale.

Even so, he was still the same handsome Liam. An ache formed in her chest. She was unable to take her eyes off him.

Seeming to sense her stare, Liam glanced up and the self-satisfied look that had covered his face fell. Before she had a chance to blink, he ducked his head and shoved a hand deep in the pocket of his jeans. His jaw clenched.

Hannah's heart kept time painfully, pumping heat to

flush up her neck and clutch at her throat. How had this happened? At least before they'd both been polite. Now they couldn't even be in the same room together.

Turning to the side, Liam walked a few seats down the length of the wooden table until he found an empty one and settled himself beside Cole. The sound of the chair scraping across the floor caused Hannah to flinch. No one seemed to notice.

The others were all talking at once, grabbing at knives and admiring the workmanship. Liam sat stiffly, refusing to look in Hannah's direction, though she still stared. She couldn't help it.

What Cookie said earlier vibrated in her mind. *You're crazy about him.* And well, yes, Hannah realized how true that was now. How true and how one sided. She was crazy, no doubt about it.

"Hey what about that bracelet you made?" Cole asked, replacing one knife on the table and trading it for another.

"What?" Liam's head whipped up, his eyes narrowing at Cole.

"I was in your place awhile back and saw it on your desk," Cole explained easily. "It might get us access to that medicine stockpile. Unless you didn't mean to trade it, of course."

"Um, yeah sure." Liam cleared his throat. Withdrawing his hand from his pocket, he produced the shining piece of silver jewelry.

As he laid it on the table, Hannah's mouth went completely dry. That was *her* bracelet. She recognized its delicate chain-links with the hand carved flowers. How many nights had she thought about it? How many times had she been on the verge of asking Liam for it?

Too many. But she never had because he'd replaced her with Lena. She figured the bracelet would go to his new girlfriend now.

It was one thing to *think* all those thoughts, and another thing entirely to *see* the damn thing winking at you from the surface of the table. He was actually going to just… what? Give it away? Like it meant nothing to him? *Because it does mean nothing to him. Just like you.*

For the span of several seconds, Hannah let her eyes zero in on the piece of jewelry. It lay there… discarded. Meaningless. And then it finally happened. Hannah's heart exploded into tiny shards inside her chest.

She tried to suck in a breath.

The air wouldn't inflate her lungs.

But what did she care about breathing anyway? Bitterness mixed with regret flowed through her. Hannah's eyes darted to Liam. He kept his gaze focused on the table. His fingers drummed along the edge. He swallowed.

Look at me!

She wanted to scream it. She wanted to get his attention, force him to see her, force him to give her something. Anything. Even if it was just a sad, *I'm sorry*. Even if it was just a confirmation of what she already knew.

But before she could make a scene, before she let a single tear fall from her eyes, she turned on her heel and strode away. On the inside, Hannah was coming all apart but pretending to be okay was what she did best.

If anyone noticed the way her hands shook as she grabbed her coat, they didn't say anything. If anyone cared that her steps were a little haphazard, that her grip on the door handle slipped just a touch, they didn't mention it.

By the time Hannah was back outside, her vision was blurring and she was gasping for air. Turning her back on the stone house and everything in it, she picked up to a run and disappeared quickly in the thick trunks of surrounding trees.

CHAPTER TWENTY-ONE_
COLE

THE SECOND COLE STEPPED FOOT OUTSIDE THE WALLS OF the compound his attention sharpened. Not that leaving Hannah behind wasn't difficult or distracting. It was. But old habits die hard. This trip into the city felt almost like another mission from Command back in the day. There was something covert about it; an added element to it that he hadn't felt in a very long time.

It was the risk. This time, he didn't want to die.

Ever since he came home to find his family in ruins on the floor of their home, a part of him had floated away. His mom and dad, his two little sisters. Shit. The sight would never leave him. After that time, every mission became like a special sort of challenge. He was driven, so to speak, to dive in deeper.

He wanted to kill. He wanted to see other men die. Someone had to pay. And if in the end he went along to his grave with them? So much the better.

The only thing keeping him from straight offing himself was Liam. His oldest, best friend and of course, the team. No matter how he may have welcomed his own death, Cole could not stomach the thought of losing a single one of his guys. In the end though, he had anyway.

But now? Well, he had Hannah to come home to. And so for the first time in years, Cole actually *wanted* to make it back. That rush of adrenaline focused him. Unlike most people, it honed his instincts.

And despite the harsh weather and grueling pace, the past six days of travel had gone off without incident. The compound and all its recent drama was behind them, well-protected, safe. No Ryder to worry over. No women to run interference on. It was nice to be on the outside, moving forward, free of the drudgery of winter's routine.

Out here, all you had to care about was where you placed your feet, who was around the next corner, how fast you could get to your gun. You gathered wood, but didn't chop it. You drank from streams, but didn't haul buckets. You slept beneath the cart or the stars. Talk was minimal.

"This the spot?" Liam pulled his horse to a stop beside Cole and glanced around.

They were in the foothills, just about to make a final descent. The flat valley below them housed what the team referred to as "the city". God knew the term was used loosely, though. Before the war, the collection of gas stations, homes and stores would've best been categorized as a mid-sized town.

But perhaps it's diminutive size and rural location were

the only reason it survived. Sure, the majority of the houses were abandoned but the band of men who controlled the borders kept the stores and their precious contents largely intact.

The place was run sort of mob-style by a man who went by the name Jensen. He was short and wiry, with calculating eyes and a heavy hand. No one crossed him. Not his own men, not visitors, or the handful of residents who kept to themselves in the surrounding suburbs.

If you wanted something, you went to him, you bargained your price and you shook hands. You never, ever went back on a handshake. But that was the thing of it… neither did Jensen. If there was honor amongst thugs, then he had it, and he demanded the same of everyone he came across.

That honor is what made the city run. That's why you could come in and trade goods, knowing, or at least feeling halfway sure, that you weren't going to be ambushed, robbed blind and killed. Jensen is what kept the place alive, so to speak. The city had some semblance of order, and it was good for all parties involved.

"Yeah, here," Cole answered finally.

Bobbing his head, he stayed put as Liam slid off his horse and signaled for the others to make camp. They would use this last little collection of trees as protection before making their final push into the city limits the following day.

All the way down, the team had kept to themselves, avoiding contact with the various other groups that lived relatively close to the compound. It would be stupid to let the others know that the majority of the team were gone on a lengthy trade trip. Instead, Cole would make certain to stop and show their faces on the way back up.

Scanning their surroundings, Cole noted the dusting of snow on the ground. A storm had blown its way over the entire mountain range two days back. They'd been slogging their way through it ever since but it was lighter here, almost gone in fact.

Glancing over his shoulder, Cole surveyed the low cloud cover that still hovered behind them. The compound must've gotten at least six inches by now. Absently, he worried about Hannah. But with a shake of his head, he dismissed the feeling. He'd left her enough wood stacked at the cabin to be comfortable. Plus he'd won the debate about leaving an extra guy behind. Between Trey, Chan and Ryder, the men at home could manage any issues that came up.

"Ya gonna get off your high horse or what?" Cookie called, causing a ripple of snickering from the team.

Cole smiled too, and slid a leg down to the ground. It was the end of another long day. Just now, he was feeling a touch tired.

All around him, camp began to take form. Small branches were being collected and thrown into a pile. The mule was being unharnessed. Bedrolls were being unloaded from the cart. Liam's horse was already unsaddled, with the man himself moving off through the trees in search of water.

That was the nice part about this area, it was wet. You were never too far from a creek, pond or spring. Stroking at the thick gray coat of his own horse, Cole walked to the cart and began to remove his animal's burdens. The gelding could use some fresh water too, and an armload of hay. All the livestock were working extra hard this winter.

Taking the heavy leather saddle in hand, Cole grunted as his eyes surveyed the cart. Normally they tossed their tack over one side to keep it up off the ground, but Liam's backpack was in the way. Grumbling under his breath, Cole stepped close to shove it aside and frowned. The damn thing was way heavier than normal.

"The hell?" Cole muttered as he set the saddle down and unzipped Liam's bag.

Inside lay what must be the entirety of Liam's personal knife collection. They were all wrapped carefully in rags or covered in leather sheaths. Feeling around, he noted a few extra portions of food and even an additional set or two of clothes.

Cole's heart jumped in his chest and he swallowed hard. So, what Cookie had been whispering about was true, Liam was leaving them. For a few good seconds, he stared at the evidence while the camp was being assembled all around him.

Losing Liam wasn't just *like* losing a brother it *was* losing a brother, at least to Cole. Hell, they'd been together since they were fucking five-years-old. Cole couldn't imagine a life without him.

Sniffing, he swiped the sleeve of his jacket under his

nose and moved fast to zip the bag back up. Damn it. Why did his chest suddenly hurt? Pressing the heel of his hand over his heart, Cole stood up. Quickly, he finished cleaning up his horse.

When he set off in search of water, he made sure to follow Liam's boot prints along the ground. Weaving in amongst the trees, Cole's eyes scanned everything around him. Though the light was dimming as night approached, he could make out a set of rabbit tracks zig zagging in the powdery white snow.

As he kept moving forward, the sound of his horse's plodding behind him filled his ears. Pushing the noise aside, he noted the crunch of his own boots, then a faint gurgling. A minute more and his eyes took in the sight before him.

Liam was crouched down, holding his canteen in the icy flow. Beside him, the bay gelding lifted his head and turned to look. Dripping a mouthful of water onto the ground, the brown horse blew air through his nostrils, then returned to his drinking.

"Hey, so I was think-" Liam began to speak before looking over his shoulder. He already knew Cole was there before he even said a word. Liam was like that, he sensed things. But then he caught sight of Cole's face and his sentence dried up on his tongue.

Clearing his throat, Liam dropped his eyes back to his canteen. In silence, he twisted on the cap and then stood up. Cole waited there, eyeing him.

Maybe if it was someone else, anyone else, he might

have been able to play this off. But the terrible truth was, he just couldn't hide his pain. Not from the boy with whom he'd shared his entire life. Not from the silent kid who'd suffered under the hand of his own father until Cole had finally said something. And not from the man who'd helped Cole to bury his parents and sisters in shallow graves in their own backyard.

"You've been going through my stuff," Liam spoke, finally turning to face him.

"Yeah." Cole shrugged.

"If you think I've taken too much from the team, then-"

"No." Cole cut him off, shaking his head ruefully. "If anything, you haven't taken enough. You'll need more. Lee, do you really think you're going to make it out there alone?"

"Truth?" Liam raised his eyebrows as Cole nodded. "I don't really care."

"Lee-"

"No." Liam's face grew hard. "Don't say anything. You don't get to say anything."

"But, Han-"

"Don't." Liam grabbed at the back of his neck before bringing his palm around to drag over his mouth. "Don't say her name. Anything you say is just you trying to keep me here and I can't. I just can't. This is my choice. My decision. Don't take it from me."

Cole bit down hard on the inside of his cheek. A slight wind picked up, twisting the tails of the two horses who stamped and itched and stepped in turn. Cole let his gray horse walk to the edge alone, dropping the lead line to drag on the ground.

Beyond the flowing creek, the slender trunks of trees spread out in the distance. Everything was smaller down here in the foothills. The collection of pines and oaks were younger, their branches more sparse. They failed to hide the shifting gray clouds that mottled the ever darkening sky.

In his head, Cole said everything that he wanted to say.

She loves you, but in her own way. The two of you are just alike, so damn stubborn, demanding and confusing. You both fight things that don't need to be fought. You fight yourselves more than anything.

What am I going to do without you? Who's going to stop me when I need to be stopped? And for that matter, who's going to stop you?

Damn. Fucking. It. Liam.

Don't you go off and die on me where I can't bury you, where I'll never know one way or the other.

But Cole kept his mouth shut. He gave Liam the respect he demanded, the respect he deserved. What was that old saying? If you love something, then let it go. Well, did that apply to a best friend? Did that apply to the only family you've got left?

Cole guessed so. He worked to swallow the lump lodged in his throat. He failed.

"Just..." Liam glanced to the side before letting his eyes jump back to Cole. "Give her back that bracelet. I made it for her, it doesn't belong anywhere else."

"Ah." Cole ducked his head.

That explained Hannah's last night of crying, he thought. And here Cole figured she was just sad he was leaving the next day. This whole situation was so twisted up. But for the first time, Cole didn't feel even a hint of jealousy at the realization. He only felt emptiness that Liam was going. He only felt the loss of a partner.

"Will you?" Liam asked again, wanting confirmation.

"Yeah." Cole cleared his throat, working to gain back his self-control. "When were you planning on leaving?"

"After we complete the trade with Jensen. I'll even come back to this spot to make sure…"

"No need." Cole shook his head. "We can part ways in the city. I'd like you at the trade deal, but after we load up, you can go your own way."

"Alright."

The two men eyed each other for a long moment. Was this really it? After everything? Then Liam stuck out his hand to shake and Cole's stomach tied itself into a knot.

Closing the distance between them, Cole took Liam's hand in his own but instead of shaking it, he pulled him in close and clapped him hard on the back. After a moment's hesitation, he felt Liam's fingers dig into his shoulder. They swayed to the side, both sniffing and refusing to break.

A few more hard slams to the back later, they separated. Cole even chanced a light laugh. Shit. Look at the two of them, full of weakness like a couple of little babies.

"Do the guys know?" Cole asked.

"Yeah," Liam admitted. "You were the last one."

Not quite the last one, Cole thought, but he didn't say it. For a fleeting second, Hannah's face passed through his mind and he wondered what her reaction would be when she found out. What would the fallout be when they all returned home and Liam wasn't with them?

By that time Liam would be so far out of reach that Hannah would never see him again. None of them would, unless Liam himself came back. Cole forced the thoughts from his mind. This wasn't the place to do this. He needed to dial himself back, he needed to remain focused.

They were out here exposed, it wasn't the time to lose his composure. Which of course is why they'd all kept it from him. Well, everyone except Cookie, but Cole hadn't wanted to believe it.

"We better get back," Cole said, stooping to retrieve his horse's rope.

Liam didn't say anything, just grunted and did the same with his own horse. Together the two men tromped back towards the cart and the smokey scent of wood burning. The fire was a risk, no doubt about it. But with their proximity to the city and the cloud cover blowing in, it was a risk they were willing to take.

Within twenty-four hours, they would be surrounded by more men than they could physically fight off. This was a game of trust, and as always… to get something, you had to give.

CHAPTER TWENTY-TWO_
LIAM

He should be feeling better. A weight should've lifted from his shoulders by now. After finally telling Cole the truth, Liam expected immediate relief. But with each step his horse took towards the city, a dark cloak seemed to wrap itself around him. Then again, the eerily quiet highway didn't help matters.

Just before dawn the team had headed down from the foothills. As the light from the sun touched the valley floor, they crossed onto the paved road. The faded black asphalt stretched for miles in either direction, but true to form, Cole avoided it until the last possible moment.

A few years back, when the crew had first come to the area, the two-lane highway had been stuffed full with vehicles. During the height of the war, a last minute mass exodus had occurred, but a wayward car wreck blocked all access. Nearly everyone was stuck there, idling until they ran out of gas.

When Liam had first seen it, there were even a few bodies left rotting along the roadway. Since that time, Jensen's men had come through and cleared most of the mess out of the way. Glancing around now, Liam shifted uncomfortably. Entering town was like an awful sort of parade.

Empty trucks and cars lined the sides of the road, their dirty windows winking in the sun as you passed. Occasionally, there was a burned out RV or a stripped trailer flipped on its side. If there was any fuel left to be had, Jensen had siphoned it out long ago.

Supposedly he was keeping it for himself. There were rumors about a handful of motorcycles hidden within the city limits but not one of them was fool enough to ask about it. There were some things better left unsaid. Knowing the wrong thing here, could get you killed.

"Think it'll work?" Liam urged his horse up alongside Cole, thinking of their plan.

"Worth a shot," Cole answered.

His friend didn't spare him a glance, keeping his gaze constantly shifting around. It wasn't that Cole was snubbing him, it was just a necessary part of the job. These visits into town were the most high risk ventures the team undertook. And now they were doing it a man short, in the off season.

It would raise questions about their crew, about their level of desperation. And the added fact that Liam wouldn't be leaving with them, well… it would only increase the curiosity. Which was why Liam had originally intended on doubling back with them, but Cole had refused.

Maybe it was a matter of pride, or maybe Cole hoped that Liam would change his mind. Whatever the reason, it saved Liam a few extra days of walking. Not that he had a particular destination in mind, but the horse would stay with the team which would leave Liam on foot.

It would be just like the good old days during the war. And the good old days is what Liam wanted. He wanted to go back to how he felt before, when the only thing he longed for was food, water and sleep. This other sort of hunger, the one that caused him to want something he couldn't have, it was making him sick.

"What if it doesn't?" Liam asked, causing Cole to reward him with a sideways glance.

"Then you'll distract him." Cole returned his gaze to the cars lining the road. "Just like we talked about already."

Liam never asked this many questions. Most of the time he didn't care about the answers. And the truth was, he didn't care about this answer either, he just wanted to hear his friend talk. Damn it, this could be the last time.

Giving up a slight nod, Liam slowed his mount and fell back. His body rocked with the motion as he watched Cole remain on point. Ace and Davey followed on foot, flanking the cart, rifles held close to their chests, heads on a swivel. Then came Cookie, who for once was riding inside the cart instead of leading the mule.

The long harness reins were draped over the animals

back with the tips coiled loosely next to Cookie's hand. The old man lay belly down facing the rear, with just his head and the tip of his weapon visible beneath a pile of blankets. One never could be too careful.

Applying a single heel to his horse's belly, Liam gently rotated the animal around until he too was surveying the land behind them. The road was vacant, you could see for a long ways off. No one moved between the empty vehicles, and they never had before.

Letting his eyes jump from the road, Liam took in the flat useless farmland that stretched along either side of the highway. There were a few old homes in the distance, but experience had taught the team that these properties were considered off limits by Jensen. No one lived there.

The wind blew cold down across the plain, but Liam hardly felt it beneath the layers of clothing and his bullet proof vest. They still had their gear from years ago, and though they rarely used the majority of it anymore, these trips to town were an exception.

With a last parting look, Liam turned his horse once more and urged him into a brisk walk. His steps clip-clopped loudly as the horse's hooves struck the road, matching the clatter from the cart and Cole's mount up ahead.

If anyone was lying in wait for them, they would be able to hear their progress from a mile away. Which of course was why Jensen had set up the entrance like this. No men lived this far out, so the only sounds coming from this direction were from visitors.

As they continued on, the vehicles became thicker, the houses cropping up more often. Before too long they were in a small suburb of sorts, surrounded by two-story houses that had once been pretty, well-tended. The remains of white picket fencing and blue painted shutters were still visible but the glass from the windows had all been removed or blown out.

If you chanced by a home with windows intact, that meant someone lived there. Though Liam gave each one a steady stare, he saw no answering signs of life. Nevertheless, the presence of other people was like an ocean undercurrent to him, steady and strong. They were being watched.

It wasn't until the team reached Main Street, with its collection of shops and darkened street signals, that the other men finally showed themselves. The hair on the back of Liam's neck stood on end and it was all he could do to keep from rubbing his palm along it. Instead, he clenched his jaw and gripped his rifle in both hands. With this horse you didn't need reins to show him where to go, so they lay looped loosely around the saddle horn.

"Well, if it isn't the hangmen crew," Jensen spoke loudly, for the benefit of his men ranged out around him. "A bit late this year, aren't we?"

Cole hated that nickname, had grumbled to Liam about it dozens of times. Of course they had earned it. Gutting and hanging men from their ankles after each kill for years was a pretty huge statement, one that worked. No one fucked with them anymore.

It didn't stop Cole from being annoyed though, not that he would show that sort of emotion here. Ever the diplomat, their fearless leader let an easy smile cross his face as he simply nodded. Liam wondered how he did it. Personally, he couldn't stand the little shit Jensen, but the wiry guy and Cole had some kind of understanding. There was a give and take of power that went on here, though it was subtle.

Jensen had five men visible by Liam's count. His eyes swiveled between them, counting. Likely there were double that positioned throughout the square. No one pointed their weapons directly at the other side, but everyone was carrying and ready.

All it would take is one wrong look and it'd be a blood bath. Somehow, Cole and Jensen always seemed to avoid it. Go figure, Liam thought, it was almost disappointing.

"Don't tell me you missed us," Cole commented, causing an indulgent chuckle to ripple through the crowd.

Swinging a leg down to the ground, he looped his rifle strap over his shoulder before stepping up to Jensen and offering a hand. For a moment, the two eyed one another and the tension ratcheted up a few notches. Liam's eyes danced to the right as he assessed the extra wide muscle that never left Jensen's side. Yeah, that one first, he thought and let his finger pulse ever so slightly against the trigger of his gun.

But then Jensen laughed and was grasping Cole's hand and the two men were shaking. The sigh that was released from the collective group was nearly audible. Every single man here had been poised to take life, but it wouldn't come to that, at least not right now.

"Will you at least be sociable this time?" Jensen asked. "How about a cup of coffee?"

Liam's mouth salivated at the thought of the bitter dark liquid. These town pricks still had a bunch of the old comforts, though by this time they ought to be running pretty low. Still, it made you wonder what else they had. People came here to trade from all around, even further south and west. But Cole never lingered, they would be in and out just the same as always.

"No, thanks," Cole gave the anticipated answer. "We haven't come to buy so much as sell. We've come across a bit of excess this year."

"Is that so?" Jensen raised his eyebrows, knowing Cole was full of shit. It was just another trade tactic. Make the other side think you don't really want anything and you've got an advantage.

Cole dipped his head casually and meandered over to the cart, his gray horse trailing him like a dog. Pulling back the blankets, he waited while Cookie got up and climbed out over the side, his rifle still clutched in his hands. Once Cookie had stepped back, Jensen made his way over with the meathead in tow and peeked over the edge. Liam didn't bother to hide his smirk as the short shit rocked up on his tiptoes to reach inside.

For the next several minutes the two men murmured

about the contents. The soap and Liam's knives, as usual, were the most coveted items. For all the farmland around, the city folk hadn't been able to keep much alive. Not a lot of excess livestock, meant not a lot of animal fat, meant no means to generate soap.

The packs of mutton jerky were also high on the list, being a different meat than they were used to getting down here. As far as the ground corn flour and pickled veggies? Those were at the bottom but still desirable.

"How're the tarps working out?" Jensen asked. The last exchange they'd made here had been more in the city's favor.

"Good," Cole conceded, then flipped a blanket back over the lot and crossed his arms over his chest. "By the time we're through, you'll have all of Liam's knives."

Jensen cracked a wide grin as he stroked along a new blade even now. The man had a thing for anything shiny or unusual. He fancied himself a king and this last vestige of the past was his personal kingdom. Liam kept his face properly bored as Jensen tilted his head up to appraise him.

"How is the good carver these days?" Jensen's smile didn't match his tone, there was hardness in it. "Hang any more works of art lately?"

Liam locked eyes with the most powerful man in the region and imagined what it would be like to draw a knife down the side of his face. Probably wouldn't take but a quick kiss with the tip before he was revealing all sorts of hidden secrets.

Ever since being with Hannah, Liam had been plagued

with a touch of shame about his violent compulsions. But looking down at Jensen now, all that evaporated. In its place came a sick sense of satisfaction. There'd been a handful of men who'd escaped the team's original sweep of the mountain. And though Liam had cursed roundly at the time, turns out they'd lived to serve a purpose. They'd lived to tell the tale.

So yeah, their team was known as the hangmen, which bothered Cole. And yeah, Liam was singled out as the cold fucker who did all the cutting. But it was all worth it. Because behind Jensen's taunting words and carefully crafted sneer of superiority... was trembling, bone deep fear.

He hid it well but the feeling sang to something inside of Liam's soul. It was a beautiful thing to behold. And just like always, Jensen was the first to blink.

"So, what is it you're after?" Jensen turned back to Cole.

"Got any salt?" Cole lead with the most sought after item, he needed a few refusals at first.

"You know we don't." Jensen sighed.

"Rice?"

"No."

"Sugar?"

At that Jensen actually laughed. Leaning forward the other man rested one hand on his knee before straightening and shaking his head. Cole kept his face serious, waiting for Jensen to settle back down. It was all part of the show.

"You've got sugar," Cole stated. "You all make the moonshine."

"We trade for the moonshine," Jensen corrected. "And if we had sugar, which I'm not saying we do, then we wouldn't be selling it."

"Fair enough." Cole shrugged, then gestured for Cookie to get back in the cart. "Looks like we wasted a trip. You'll want to put that knife back."

Jensen frowned at that, glancing down at the new blade in his hand. Running a thumb over the edge, he shifted his shoulders and seemed to be thinking something over. Meanwhile, Cookie crossed back to the cart and made to climb over the side.

"Wait, wait." Jensen lifted his head. "What else are you looking for? We've come across some boots. We've got a fair amount of pig meat."

He's got him, Liam thought, his fingers curling almost imperceptibly around his weapon. Now here comes Cole's part.

"Boots, huh?" Cole rolled his shoulders and scratched at his head. "Got any winter clothes? New jeans? Jackets?"

"Well, everyone's running low on that kind of stuff," Jensen protested, but he was on the hook now, he wanted to make a deal.

"What about needle and thread? Any material?" Cole was dancing around actually asking for what they really wanted. Liam held his breath.

"Some needle and thread, yeah, but no material." Jensen paused, thinking.

Come on, Liam coaxed in his mind, just let that little pea brain work you greedy bastard. Cole remained silent, waiting.

"But we've got all those extra women's clothes," Jensen volunteered, his face brightening at his own cleverness. "You could use that as material, cut it down and sew it back up to make it bigger."

"Women's clothes?" Cole let a sneer cross his face, but inside Liam knew he was dancing a freaking jig. Yes, they needed women's clothes, but no one could know why. Not the real reason.

"Beggars can't be choosy," Jensen countered. "You could look them over, see what you think."

"Oh, alright, we'll look them over," Cole conceded. "How much pork did you say you have?"

After that, Liam tuned out. Letting his gaze travel around the square, he assessed each man in turn. From their prior encounters, he guessed they were all locals to the area from before the war. They had a mix of weathered faces with shaggy beards and jaded eyes. Most were a decade or two older than he, probably escaping the draft due to age or maybe ducking off the grid and avoiding the whole disaster altogether.

The handful that appeared younger might have been ex-soldiers like themselves. Maybe they'd been passing through at one point and decided to stay. Either way, they were Jensen's now and their origins didn't really matter.

Liam knew for a fact that Jensen traded with former Southie Soldiers on occasion. Did it grate on him? Trading with the enemy? Nah. Not really.

At this point, the war was over. The world was destroyed and no one could afford the luxury of choosing a side. All that remained were men you were with, and men you weren't with. Loyalty didn't extend further than that.

After Jensen and Cole finished with their negotiation, the whole lot of them moved a few buildings further down Main Street. Stopping the cart in front of an old store with boarded up windows, Liam watched intently as Jensen's men steadily unloaded the cart.

They would take all of it, like they always did. Every knife, every package of food, everything. Bundle after bundle was lifted up and carried the few steps along the cement sidewalk and through the propped open glass door of the shop.

Glancing up to the sign above the door, Liam read the words, *Evelyn's Books and Coffee*. For the briefest moment he wondered who Evelyn was, imagining the store when it first opened. In his vision he saw the space filled with books, the smell of coffee and the murmur of quiet people in the morning.

But then the spell was broken and he was sucked back to reality, surrounded by death and destruction. There was no electricity providing light. There were no cars cruising down the street, no more customers with their credit cards and their petty worries. Evelyn was dead. All her female friends were dead, or maybe imprisoned in a collection of fortresses around the world.

Liam let the darkness inside of him overflow in his body once more. He had fought it before, ever since Hannah had come into his life, he had battled with it and even won. But that only lasted for a few fleeting months, and there was no point to it anymore.

This soul sucking blackness left him with a familiar empty feeling. Numbness. Blessed nothing. He welcomed it, for the relief he had sought had finally come back to him. There was a certain comfortable steadiness in caring about no one, especially yourself. A small smile creased the corners of his lips and Liam even let out the tiniest sigh. None of it mattered anymore, he was free.

When the cart was empty, the team moved even further into town. Jensen's group kept pace with them, never showing more than five men at once. It was meant to be reassuring, and maybe for other groups, it worked. But for their team, it was almost patronizing.

Did Jensen actually think they hadn't done their home-work? Did he actually think they hadn't taken the time to surveil them? In the past, they'd spent weeks hiding in the surrounding hills, doing just that. Hunting, watching, counting, tracking.

For what it was worth, Jensen did have salt. He did have sugar. He did make the moonshine. He had between forty and fifty men under his direct command at any given time and another twenty who lived in the outskirts.

Sitting back just a touch in the saddle, Liam slowed his

horse and watched the others range ahead. One more block over and the buildings opened up to reveal a massive parking lot with silver street lamps standing guard over another collection of useless vehicles. At the far end was the single biggest building the town had to offer, the old Wal Mart in all its capitalist glory.

Inside, there were aisles and aisles of commercial goods. Clothing, groceries, supplies of all sorts. It was the most secure, most heavily guarded place in the entire area and their team was about to go shopping inside.

Circling around to the rear entrance, Cole stood beside Jensen as two of his men bent to lift the large rolling metal door. The team would take the mule and cart through the loading bay and all the way into the center of the store. Once inside, Jensen typically observed each and every item that the team took, making certain it was all a part of their original negotiation.

This time, however, Cole and Liam had other plans for the little shit. As Liam observed, Cole leaned in to whisper to Jensen, then tipped his chin over his shoulder. Jensen's eyes followed and locked on Liam, who sat resolutely still on his horse. After a beat, Jensen bobbed his head and the two of them walked over. Cole's face was cloudy, they were nearing the end.

"This guy tells me you're parting ways," Jensen began, his head tipped up.

"That's right," Liam acknowledged.

Swinging his leg over the side of his horse, Liam dismounted and grabbed for Cole's reins along with his own. Before Jensen knew what was happening, Cole turned his back on them both and motioned for the team to enter the building.

"Are you planning on sticking around?" Jensen asked, absorbed completely in the very real possibility that he would have a knife-wielding psycho haunting his city.

"Just passing through," Liam assured him. "But I might need to stay on the outskirts tonight. Any rules about that?"

Jensen let out a huff of breath and brought the tip of his new knife up to scratch gently at his forehead. His eyes were intelligent as they assessed Liam, and this close up he appeared about late-fifties in age. There were wrinkles working around the corners of his eyes, though Liam was certain they all likely had these signs of stress now, regardless of age.

For a minute or more, Jensen stared. It didn't unnerve Liam in the least. He was used to this sort of scrutiny. In fact, he almost enjoyed the silent exchange. Because unlike most men, Liam had nothing at all to prove and he had nothing at all to hide.

Peering into the soul of another man, glimpsing his thoughts and hidden impressions, it was priceless really. It gave Liam an advantage, and maybe that was one reason why he would survive this. Because now he knew for certain that Jensen and his men would be coming for him tonight.

Another man might be afraid, but Liam welcomed it. Let them come, he thought, let them all come to me.

"It's going to cost you," Jensen said finally. "Got anything I want?"

"I've got another knife you may be interested in, but that seems steep for one night of protection." Liam let a slow smile creep across his face. "Got any moonshine to throw in?"

CHAPTER TWENTY-THREE_
HANNAH

Hovering over the cast iron pot, Hannah concentrated on the water, waiting for the moment it began to boil. There's only so much you can do with mutton, pickled carrots and corn flour. After a while it doesn't matter how you mix the ingredients, everything tastes awful.

Tonight would be different though. Hannah had spent all day rummaging around in the cellar of the storage building and was determined to make something new.

"Smells good." Ryder came up to lean against the wall, that same silly smile stretching across his face.

"I just hope it *is* good," Hannah countered. "And you can't smell anything yet, it's only water."

Ryder blushed, then laughed good-naturedly when Hannah reached up to pat teasingly at his cheek. It didn't matter that she didn't feel like smiling. It didn't matter that all she really wanted to do was curl up in Cole's bed and cover her head with the blankets.

All that mattered was putting on a bright face and getting the job done. So that's what Hannah did. She put everything she had into making their meals.

Behind her, Flynn and Trey were playing cards at the long table. Their stream of banter seemed so subdued compared to the normal noise level of the stone house. The guys had only been gone for three days, but already it felt like a lifetime.

"Can I help?" Ryder asked.

"Sure," Hannah sighed, placing both hands on her hips. "You can open these cans of peas."

"Alright."

Ryder stepped around her and grabbed the metal opener off one of the shelves. While Hannah diced a few potatoes into tiny cubes, Ryder chatted about the shift in weather. Snow was coming. Probably a whole lot of it.

Hannah let his voice filter in the background of her mind and focused on the task at hand. It wasn't hard to tune him out. They all knew a big storm was blowing in. An icy cold wind had picked up yesterday and a gathering line of imposing gray clouds could be seen edging closer from the west.

Would the guys be caught up in it? Was Cole prepared to handle that kind of snow? And for that matter was Liam? Hannah's gut dropped at the thought of him, and her hand stilled a moment while clutching her knife.

The little red handle felt so smooth in her palm, it was a

taunting reminder. She'd do almost anything to go back to the day Liam had given it to her. But the world didn't work like that. You didn't get to go back.

With a pop, Ryder set the first can down on the wooden work table and reached for the other. Hannah glanced over at the pot and noted the steam drifting from the rim. It was ready.

Scooping up a handful of potato bits she dropped them into the boiling water. Her goal for the meal was to end up with a rich soup of some kind. Thankfully the goat was still producing and had delivered a quarter bucket of milk just that morning.

Running the back of her wrist along her forehead, Hannah brushed her hair out of her face. It was warm standing beside the fireplace and perspiration gathered at her brow. The long sleeves of her shirt were rolled up to her elbows and her jacket lay discarded over an empty chair. That only served to lessen the intensity of the heat, not get rid of it entirely.

Since the others had gone, the chores had stacked up quickly and Hannah welcomed the distraction. Each morning, she doled out hay to the livestock before beginning a day filled with meal prep, hauling water and scrubbing dishes. At this point she relished the opportunity to keep busy, to stay occupied. To keep her brain from drifting.

The front door slammed open. Hannah jumped in surprise at the sound and turned to look. Her heart leapt in her chest and, for the briefest moment, she found herself wishing it was Liam or Cole.

But no, it was only Chan. The force of the wind had ripped the wooden door from his grasp.

Darkness was falling outside, she could see its deep purple hue filling the doorway. Before she turned back to the fire, Hannah spied Lena. She was always trailing Chan now. She even sat through watch duty with him.

They were just done with their watch shift now, in fact. But with only two men able to climb the ladder, they were spread pretty thin. Even so, there were only two times no one was on duty, breakfast and dinner.

"Anything else?" Ryder's question broke through Hannah's reverie.

"No, I think that does it." Hannah offered him a smile. "You can tell the others it should be ready in a bit."

"Got it." Ryder bobbed his head happily before crossing the room to join in the card game.

Returning her attention to the large pot, Hannah pulled it off the direct flame before adding a pinch of salt. She didn't dare use too much. Cookie was liable to kill her when he got back and saw what all she had used already. In her defense though, Hannah planned on making butter and a sort of creamy spread while they were gone. Hopefully the new products would offset everything else.

After several minutes, she dumped in the cans of peas and then waited a bit longer before adding the milk. Stirring the concoction idly, Hannah did a dangerous thing, she let her mind drift. Soon she was back in Liam's cabin, with his eyes staring at her and her back pressed into his desk.

Giving her head a sharp shake, she fought against the memory and the feelings it brought on. Then the image was morphing. She was facing the desk now, looking down. Her hand traced over that silver bracelet.

"Ow," Hannah gasped and pressed the heel of one hand to her temple. The pain came on hot and fast, like an electric jolt to her brain. Sucking in a breath, Hannah opened her eyes, but the room she saw was not Liam's cabin.

She was standing in the doorway to an office, his office. The space before her was dark, and for the first time she realized it had no windows. Glancing up to the corner of the room, she noted the little light on the camera was still a steady red. For a beat, she battled pure fear.

Swallowing hard, Hannah raised her voice. "Dr. B?"

Silence.

"Dr. Bartholomew, are you in here?" Hannah pushed the rest of the way through the door and reached along the wall for a light. It took the slam of the door closing behind her before she realized there was no switch. Her heart picked up the pace, but she didn't want to leave without answers.

"The others have some questions." Hannah stepped further into the space. "They don't like some of the mandates. There's been a lot of talk about forming a sort of counsel... with a voting board. Dr. B?"

Another few steps would bring her to the center of the room.

Hannah held her breath and stood perfectly still. This was not like him. He never sat in the dark like this. Why would Dr. B send for her if he wasn't here?

"I can't see a thing," Hannah said finally. "I wish you would turn on a light."

But in the next moment, Hannah wanted to take back those words. As if by magic, the overhead lights switched on, and Hannah slapped both hands over her mouth to keep from screaming.

There before her, slumped forward in his office chair, sat Dr. Bartholomew. The darkened computer screen in front of him was splattered with streaks of blackish-blood. His head was turned to one side as it lay on his keyboard, his face caved in on itself... or maybe just blown all apart.

He shot himself, Hannah thought, her gaze darting to the black handgun that lay discarded on the floor.

"Why?" Hannah's voice came out strangled. "What are we supposed to do now?"

She took a tentative step back, her whole body trembling. But just before she turned to run, the pager at her side buzzed. Glancing down at the message, her heart stopped and her blood ran cold.

"Hey, Hannah Mae," Lena's voice was quiet but steady. It sounded close to her ear. "Are you alright?"

"What?" Hannah coughed once, and was sucked back into the present.

"You were out of it," Lena explained. "You almost fell."

"Oh."

Hannah blinked a few times before Lena's worried face came into focus. The other woman had her hands bracing either side of Hannah's arms. Just behind her, Chan stood watching.

"I just..." Hannah trailed off, her mind was taking its time coming back to full force.

"Another headache?" Lena supplied, the expression on her face was reassuring and calm.

"Yes."

Hannah ducked her head as the other woman's hands fell back to her sides. The others were all staring, the room had gone completely still.

"This looks delicious," Lena said, gesturing to the bubbling soup. "Is it ready?"

"Um." Hannah glanced over her shoulder before swiping a trembling hand across her upper lip. "Yeah. Yes, it's finished."

"Let me help you serve then." Lena offered her a gentle smile.

Nodding automatically, Hannah backed away a few steps and watched as Lena and Chan went to work. They took down six ceramic bowls with big silver spoons, the handles of which were etched with a swirling ivy. The creamy soup with its green peas and potatoes splattered and splashed just a bit as it poured from the metal ladle into each dish.

Lena handed the servings to Chan who carried them to the long table where everyone seemed determined to focus on their meal. When the last bowl had been transferred over, Lena took Hannah by the hand and led her to sit beside them.

Her grasp felt warm and dry against the sweat lining Hannah's palm. It was the first physical contact she had had with anyone since the morning Cole left. The simple exchange had tears forming in the back of her eyes.

They were all going to let her get away with it. No one was going to question her about the headaches or her memory. At the realization, Hannah was grateful. She knew in her heart that she owed them an explanation, but letting her mind go back to that scene... she wasn't ready for it. At least not yet.

The talk over dinner was idle when it resumed. Even Flynn restricted her comments to the team's stockpile of herbs and the potential for making natural remedies. Her latest project was a small greenhouse. Ryder and Trey were on board and had been checking the compound for materials.

They wouldn't be able to break ground on it until spring, but if Flynn could get a garden going, then their ability to produce not only herbs but a variety of vegetables would increase. It was a good idea, one that Hannah hoped would work out, though she didn't say as much.

Near the end of the meal, when empty bowls were scraped clean and shoved out of the way, Trey stood up and stretched. It was his turn for watch duty and though the storm was coming, he wanted to get a good last look before they were socked in.

Slinging his rifle over his shoulder, the others murmured a few parting words before he was off. Hannah rose next. Collecting the dirty dishes in her arms, she carried them back to the fire. She always kept a bucket of water warming and a bar of soap on the shelf. For a sponge, she used small squares of old rags.

A clean stack of them lay neatly folded nearby and as Hannah dumped the bowls and spoons into the water, she grabbed for one. Some might turn their nose up at the prospect of scrubbing dishes, but Hannah found the activity comforting in a way. She liked the isolation it provided her; that, and the satisfaction of a completed task.

Tonight though, she would have help. Lena came to stand beside her, carefully drying and stacking without uttering a word. This was typical of them, Hannah now knew. She'd gotten flashes of them quietly working side by side back in their shared apartment.

They'd often folded laundry together too, their shared silence interrupted only by the occasional giggle. What lovely secrets had the two of them shared? Hannah still couldn't bring that part to mind.

"You okay?" Lena kept her voice low.

"Yeah."

"You want to talk about it?"

"I don't know if I can," Hannah answered honestly, swallowing just a bit.

"You're remembering things," Lena stated, but there was no accusation in her tone.

"Yes," Hannah admitted. "This last flashback was…"

Trailing off, Hannah searched for the right word. Painful? Terrifying? As she thought about it, her hands stilled, clutching the damp rag. She needed to find her brother, needed to find him bad.

"It's okay." Lena reached out, laying a hand over Hannah's own. "I just want to be friends again. Can we be friends?"

Hannah blinked, tilting her head down to watch as Lena loosened the rag from her grip. Taking it smoothly, she wrung out the water and set it aside to dry.

"Yes," Hannah answered, finally. "I would like that."

"Then let us help you." Lena gestured to Chan who was never very far from her side. "Let's walk down to your place, maybe we can make some tea?"

Hannah's eyebrows shot up in surprise at the suggestion. They did have plenty of pine trees around, the needles were good for tea, and she had two fresh water buckets at home. It might take a while to heat but it'd go quicker if they borrowed the old copper tea pot from the storage building.

"That would be…" Hannah felt a tingle cruise through her blood stream. "Really nice."

"Great." Lena smiled before nodding to Chan who bobbed his head.

While Hannah shrugged into her coat, Chan dumped the dirty dish water outside, then circled back to grab his own jacket and help Lena into hers. With a few parting goodbyes to the others, the three of them stepped out into the first falling flakes of snow. The wind had subsided and the crystal clear night was so quiet and peaceful.

Holding out her hand as she walked, Hannah caught a few fat flakes in her palm. It was truly beautiful. The darkness mixed with the gentle falling of snow and the crunch of their boots on the ground. Lena leaned into Hannah, playfully bumping her shoulder with her own.

Glancing sideways at the dark-haired woman, Hannah found herself giving up a small laugh. This was right. This felt normal. Maybe it would be okay to finally tell someone. Maybe it would be okay to confess all the mix of memories. Lena had known her for years, perhaps she could help straighten some things out.

At the bottom of the hillside, Hannah paused by a low hanging pine bough and picked off a handful of needles. The tea wasn't the best tasting in the world, but it wasn't terrible either. Plus Flynn had mentioned it was high in vitamin C, which was good since they didn't have access to hardly any fruit.

"We could use the tea pot in the storage building," Hannah suggested, looping her elbow in the crook of Lena's arm. "Right Chan?"

"Sure," Chan replied, happy to trail the two women as they passed Cole's cabin.

Coming to a stop at the wooden door of the storage building, Hannah glanced up. The snow was falling all around them now, coming down in swift fat flakes. Overhead, the low clouds were luminous, filling with a backlight from the moon that lingered above them. Before Lena could reach for the handle, Chan stepped around her and pulled the door open himself. It creaked slightly on its hinges, but the sound was soft, like the last tones of a lullaby.

And if only they could've stayed there together, frozen in time, knowing nothing but the impending sweetness of good company and a hot cup of tea. But it wasn't to be. Hannah's confession to Lena, their renewed friendship, Chan's quiet steady presence. It would never come to pass.

In the next moment, there was the rapid release of gunfire. A shrill whistle followed, sending a lightening bolt of fear to shoot through Hannah's body.

"Get inside!" Chan shoved them both hard over the threshold, before slamming the door shut. "Stay down!"

"Chan, no!" Lena called, but Hannah held onto the other woman's wrist, keeping her from following him out the door.

Pop. Pop. Pop. Pop.

The rifle sounded again, then they could hear another piercing whistle. Then more shots.

They were so close. The sounds were echoing and harsh and loud. Hannah could feel the gunfire take over the rhythm of her heart. What was happening? Something was coming… or someone.

Hannah sucked in a breath and backed away a step. The sounds of men shouting filled the air.

"We have to hide," Hannah hissed, tugging Lena further into the building. "We have to find somewhere to hide."

THE MOONSHINE BURNED. SMACKING HIS LIPS TOGETHER, Liam held the glass jar back from his face before giving his head a shake. It burned all the way down. In fact, his whole throat felt like it was coated in fire, but then in the next moment, it was gone. Better have another sip, he thought, he wasn't nearly drunk enough.

Leaning back against his rolled up sleeping bag, Liam took another swig and stared at the fire. Was it reckless of him to build it so close to the city? Maybe. Okay, yes it was. But that was the beauty of it all, Liam no longer cared.

He'd done his part and now he was free. Right? That's what this huge empty hole in his chest was made of... freedom.

And shit, the plan had gone off without a hitch. Liam had kept little old Jensen by his side, selecting moonshine and taunting him with flashy knives until the team emerged from the Wal Mart unscathed. Though Liam hadn't seen it for himself, he knew that inside the cart, buried beneath a layer of pillows and blankets, was the true objective of their mission.

Women's clothing. And not just the biggest stuff that would convert best into men's clothing, no. Women's clothes in all the correct sizes, complete with bras and underwear, socks and shoes. Without Jensen and his calculating, intelligent eyes, the team had been able to go inside with only a handful of dumb guards to watch. They were supposed to be in the women's section anyway, per the negotiation that everyone had listened to, so there was no question as to why the team lingered there.

Clearing his throat, Liam leaned forward, bracing his elbows on his knees. He had definitely done the right thing. Sure it had felt like a sock to the gut the way Cole had left, only nodding his head before turning to go.

But they'd been surrounded by Jensen and his men at the time. The goodbyes that needed to be said had been spoken already. So of course there were no last second parting words, no slaps on the back. Liam simply handed over the reins to the horses, grabbed his bedroll and pack and stepped away.

Watching his brothers all head in the opposite direction wasn't something he wanted to do specifically. It was something he had to do. He waited to make sure they were all clear. He waited until the tip of Cookie's rifle gleamed in the distance before turning on his heel and heading out.

Jensen hadn't said anything to him either. Liam shouldered his packs, clutched his cold black weapon in his hands and walked quietly down the street. No one bothered him, though he felt their eyes tracking him all the while.

And those eyes had kept pace with him as he moved through the city, down paved streets lined with gutted gas stations and restaurants. Past a small two-story motel that had once housed tourists and hunting parties alike. Hell, Liam could feel them all the way to the outskirts, where the property stretched along with barbed wire fencing and the occasional ranch house.

That was when he'd left the road, stepping casually into the overgrown fields. The eyes stopped then. Liam could feel them ease back into the distance as he crossed an old wooden bridge.

Smart Liam would have kept right on going. Smart Liam would have hiked for the tree line, then up higher into the hills. He would've circled back using the cover of darkness and stayed up all night, watching. But Smart Liam had been replaced by Free Liam. And damned if Free Liam wasn't a bit of a cocky drunk.

So here he sat, beneath a twisted old oak with a raging fire throwing light for miles. Laughing to himself, Liam tipped back another shot of alcohol and welcomed the buzz that permeated his brain. It'd been so long since he'd done anything like this. He only hoped he'd get a chance to wet his blade before it was all through.

Clearing his throat, Liam set the jar of moonshine on the ground beside him and rummaged through his bag. He pulled out a hunk of mutton and his longest carving knife.

Casually, he began to shave off whisper thin slices and pop them into his mouth.

The meat never had tasted this good before. Must be the others watching him now that made it better. The impending death all around him that made life that much sharper… more acute.

"Can I help you gentlemen?" Liam raised his voice but didn't stop what he was doing.

"We saw the fire." Jensen stepped into the light.

"I paid to stay the night," Liam reminded him as seven additional men shifted closer.

"Yeah." Jensen ran a finger down the edge of his own knife. "You did."

"How do you like it?" Liam asked.

"Hmm?"

"The knife. How do you like it?"

"Oh, this thing?" Jensen gave the blade a quick toss before catching it easily by the handle. "It's maybe your best yet."

Liam just smiled at that, a true Cheshire Cat grin that spread naturally across his face. Without saying anything more, he continued to carve off slices of meat and pop them neatly into his mouth.

For a few moments more, they all watched him. The fire crackled and spit a few sparks as an old log twisted and collapsed.

A curl worked its way deep in Liam's belly, tightening and tightening all the while as he chewed. His heart hammered a bit, but his palms were completely dry.

Absently, he fingered the broad knife in his hand. He figured given half a chance, he would at least take Jensen down with him.

"Would you like to sit?" Liam asked, finally.

When Jensen nodded his head and crouched by the fire, it was all Liam could do to keep his mouth from dropping open in surprise. Though unexpected the move may be, Liam held his composure with a straight face. Where was the attack? They should've gone for him by now.

Setting the meat aside, Liam laid his knife in his lap but kept hold of it with one hand. The jar of moonshine glinted out of the corner of his eye and with a shrug of his shoulders, he reached for it and took yet another chug.

"Ah." Liam smacked his lips and let loose a whistle. "Want some?"

"I'll take a bit." Jensen reached for the jar and gulped a swallow down.

Well, isn't this a nice little picnic. The fuck do you want Jensen? Though he wanted to ask the question aloud, Liam knew better.

Even half-crocked and filled with adrenaline, the interrogator inside of him was an exacting master. And the great questioner would be the one dictating this game, whether he was drunk or not. There was something extra playing out here that Liam hadn't anticipated. Jensen wanted something from him, something other than a simple killing.

Curious, Liam took the jar back and set it on the ground between them, then let his gaze dance around the circle of men. Only one of them looked him in the eye, the wide-necked beast from before. All the rest stared at things around Liam, or even on Liam, but not at Liam.

They're scared, he realized. The vast majority of these men were afraid of him. Any other time in his life, Liam would've felt gleeful at the realization. It meant he could more than likely fight his way out of this mess and survive. But for some reason he suddenly felt a defeated sort of disappointment instead.

Tilting his head back to look at the sky, Liam let loose a long sigh.

"What do you want, Jensen?"

"So, you break up with your boyfriend?"

Liam's head snapped back. Eyes scanning, he analyzed Jensen's serious face before a sharp laugh escaped him. *Boyfriend?* After a second though, he really thought about the question and frowned. The other man really wasn't so far off the mark was he?

"Fuck off." Liam spat into the fire before taking another shot.

"Because if you're into that sort of thing, we've got that here."

"Oh, yeah?" Liam looked pointedly at the biggest guy there and then back at Jensen. When the other man merely shrugged, Liam shook his head and stared at the fire. "No thanks, I'm just passing through."

"It's changing out there," Jensen cautioned. "A lot of factions are building up. We could use a guy of your... talents. You could make a nice life here."

That's the thing, Liam thought, I'm not interested in a nice life. Fingering the knife in his lap, Liam watched the flames dance. It was a good sized fire, one that threw heat in a fairly wide ring. Already some of the others were having to step back, they couldn't stand the heat. The tips of Liam's boots caught the reflection and it mesmerized him for several moments.

"What other factions?" He asked finally, might as well know what he was walking into.

"There's a big one further southwest." Jensen eased back to sitting, his legs propped up in front of him. "Guy that runs it came through here about a year ago now. He was alone at the time and I didn't think much of him."

"But now he's a big deal?"

Jensen shifted uncomfortably before rolling his shoulders and huffing a dismissive breath. Maybe he wanted his men to believe that he didn't feel threatened by this group in the southwest, but Liam now knew for a fact that he was.

"He makes promises he can't keep," Jensen explained. "Men come from everywhere to listen to him talk, then they stay. It's like he's amassing some sort of army."

"What sort of promises?"

"The women kind." Jensen chuckled knowingly and the sentiment was echoed around by a few of his men. "He says there are thousands of women living in some kind of metal fortress."

"Is that so?" Liam's pulse kicked up, pushing the alcohol-laced blood through his system. If he hadn't been so drunk, then maybe he would've been able to keep his hand from shaking. "This guy have a name?"

"Yeah." Jensen reached for the moonshine and took another swig. When he set the jar back down, he blew out a hot breath before glancing over at Liam. "He goes by the name, Linfield. Uriah Linfield."

CHAPTER TWENTY-FIVE_
COLE

COLE HADN'T BEEN THIS TIRED IN A LONG, LONG TIME. Every muscle in his body was aching and every bone for that matter. The snow was falling heavily all around him now, coating the ground in a thick winter's blanket. It served as a painful reminder why they never traveled this time of year.

About a foot of it was already stacked up on the ground, making the effort of hauling the cart up the grade that much more challenging. At the base of the mountain, Cole had dismounted and hitched both horses next to the mule. Between the three animals, the cart was moving steadily, but not without effort.

With a fresh gust of wind, some snow picked up from the ground and swirled in a tiny turning tornado before settling back down. Tilting his face up, Cole could just make out the final twists in the narrow roadway. They were almost home and had gotten everything they went out for.

Well… unless you counted Liam. Cole huffed a breath. Trying not to let his sense of foreboding get the better of him.

Thanks to the weather, he hadn't had much time to think about leaving his best friend behind. Talk around their fires at night had been brief and the entire team seemed to agree on one point. Liam made his choice, it was his right and that was that.

"Almost there boys!" Cole shouted the words over his shoulder, though he wasn't sure he'd be heard by everyone.

Their plan of meeting with some of the local groups on their way back up had been thwarted by the storm. It would've taken a few extra days to loop through the various territories and everyone had agreed it would be best to bypass them this time.

The team all just wanted to get home already. Home to roaring fires, hot food and the voices of their women. *Their women.* The phrase felt so good it almost warmed Cole just to think it. He missed Hannah. He ached for her in fact, but there was also an edge to it. He knew he was bringing pain along with him.

She was the one person Liam hadn't said goodbye to and now Cole was left having to do it. Damn it. The phrase echoed dully in his mind but he couldn't summon any anger to go along with the words, only a sense of loss.

With each forward step Cole's tall brown boots sunk

deeper in the snow. He was thankful they were waterproof, at least being a soldier had provided him with that much.

Up ahead, the outline of their gate appeared, covered in white powder. The wind caused it to sway ever so slightly on its hinges and the movement caught Cole's eye.

Letting out a shrill whistle, he announced their arrival. Silence. No answer.

That's not all that surprising though, Cole assured himself. No one would be standing watch in this heavy of a storm, you couldn't see more than a few yards in front of your face.

Glancing behind him, Cole watched the others trudging doggedly along, hands stuffed deep in their pockets. He wasn't quite sure what time it was, the sun hadn't made an appearance in over four days. If forced to guess, Cole would've been able to narrow it down only between day and night. It wasn't pitch black, so therefore it must be sometime during the day.

That meant Hannah was probably awake, maybe even cooking something right this moment. Cole's stomach rumbled and he picked up the pace. Closing the distance to the gate, he reached for the metal chain that kept it closed and came up short. It was gone. The gate wasn't locked.

Giving the gate a shove, he watched it swing slowly inward, bouncing a bit on its hinges under the burden of snow. *That's not right.*

Cole fought against the surge of adrenaline that spiked inside of him. Maybe the guys had needed the chain for something… to secure something in the storm. Yeah, that was reasonable. Wasn't it?

"What's the hold up?" Cookie grumbled, having stopped beside Cole who stood dumbly in the road.

"Chain's gone."

Cole gave the others a quick glance before stepping further into the compound. No one said a word. No one tried to make an excuse. And it was suddenly so damn quiet.

All that could be heard was the whisper of wind moving through the thick trees. Cole's breathing automatically slowed down as he ripped his rifle off his shoulder and clutched it in his hands.

Picking up his feet, he did his best to jog quickly through the snow. Each step was a hopping sort of struggle though, the stuff was so deep. It made everything harder, the snow.

But then he was falling forward, tripping and stumbling until he landed on his knees and elbows in the white powder. His toe had caught on something.

Sitting back, Cole looked down. What he saw had his heart hammering inside his chest, he could feel the thumping against his ribs.

"No." Cole tossed his weapon down and started to dig. "No. No. No."

The others were beside him now, helping him. Handful after handful of the icy white crystals were shoved aside. The guys were all kneeling and cursing, helping to unearth the frozen body.

Finally, Cole was able to roll the man onto his back. Chan. *No.* It was fucking Chan with those brown eyes staring off, eyelashes frozen with ice.

"Fuck!" Cole lunged forward, grabbing his weapon before shoving up.

Then he ran.

He took off as fast as he could go, with the rest of them just behind. Waving his hand above his head, he motioned for two to loop up to the left while he and another would stay low and right. He didn't care who went where, he didn't look back to see.

Rifle poised to fire, Cole's lungs burned with heat while his body went completely numb. *Hannah.* The word kept repeating itself over and over in his mind. *Hannah. Hannah.*

A word from the author:

Don't worry, don't worry.
No more cliffhangers… I promise! You'll get satisfaction
with the third book in the series… Get Book 3 right now:
SURVIVING THE WALL

Join my email list…
LK MAGILL NEWSLETTER
Join my ARC Team!
Click on the link - ARC TEAM - LK MAGILL

Reviews, pretty please…
Each and every positive review makes a huge difference.
Be it Amazon, Kobo, iBooks, Barnes and Noble; no matter
the retailer, I read and appreciate them all.
Thank you and I hope to see you in the future.

Websites:
www.lkmagill.com

Like me on Facebook:
https://fb.me/LKMagill1

Follow me on Instagram:
https://www.instagram.com/lk.magill.author

Check out my Amazon page:
http://amazon.com/author/lkmagill

Standalone novels:

VANISH ME

The Captive Series:

THE CAPTIVE BORN - Book One

THE CAPTIVE MISSING - Book Two

THE CAPTIVE RISING - Book Three

Outlasting Series:

OUTLASTING AFTER - Book One

CHASING TRUTH - Book Two

SURVIVING THE WALL - Book Three

BREAKING BEFORE - Book Four

TAKING TOMORROW - Book Five

FINDING FOREVER - Book Six